A DANGEROUS PLAN

DISCARD

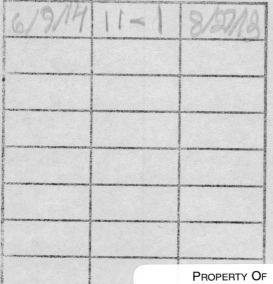

A Dangerous Plan

20

LEFT BEHIND

>THE KIDS<

Jerry B. Jenkins

Tim LaHaye

WITH CHRIS FABRY

TYNDALE KiDS

TYNDALE HOUSE PUBLISHERS, INC.
WHEATON, ILLINOIS

Visit Tyndale's exciting Web site at www.tyndale.com

Discover the latest Left Behind news at www.leftbehind.com

Edited by Curtis H. C. Lundgren

Published in association with the literary agency of Alive Communications, Inc., 7680 Goddard Street, Suite 200, Colorado Springs, CO 80920.

ISBN 0-8423-4314-8, mass paper

Printed in the United States of America

08 07 06 05 04 03 02
9   8   7   6   5   4   3   2   1

To Brandon James

TABLE OF CONTENTS

What's Gone On Before

JUDD Thompson, Jr. and the rest of the Young Tribulation Force are involved in the adventure of a lifetime. The global vanishings have left them alone, and now another judgment has fallen from God.

Judd, who has been on a missions trip to Africa with Mr. Stein, is flying back to Israel. As the plane breaks through a dark cloud that covers the earth, demon locusts attack.

Lionel Washington and his new friend Sam Goldberg await Judd at the airport. Suddenly, a swarm of locusts descend on the terminal. Lionel closes a door to keep the beasts out.

Mark Eisman is in Kankakee, Illinois, to meet Carl Meninger, a friend of his cousin John. As the locusts fly at them, Mark finds an abandoned car and pushes Carl inside. Mark explains the truth about God and what is happening. Carl prays and is miraculously spared being stung by the locusts.

At the schoolhouse, Vicki Byrne prepares for the worst and gets the unbelievers into a sealed room downstairs. A new woman, Lenore, has arrived with her baby, Tolan.

When the locusts attack, Janie is stung and writhes in pain. Later, Vicki hears screams and runs downstairs to find Shelly and Darrion struggling to keep the locusts out. A locust burrows into the room and heads straight for the crib where the baby, Tolan, is sleeping.

Join the kids as they try to convince their friends of the truth and struggle to survive the most horrifying judgment yet.

ONE

The Vicious Attack

VICKI Byrne lunged for the crib and swung a board at the hovering locust. She missed, but the beast veered away, screaming, "Apollyon!"

"More are trying to get in!" Darrion yelled.

"Stay there," Vicki said. "I'll get this one!"

The locust dove at the baby again. Vicki's stomach turned at the hideous face of the creature. She swung again and connected. The locust bounced off the wall and fell into the crib.

"Don't let it hurt my baby!" Lenore yelled from above.

"Shut the door!" Vicki said, peeking over the edge of the crib. The baby cried and kicked at his cover as the locust lay a few inches from his feet.

"It's OK, Tolan," Vicki said. "I'm going to get this bad thing away from you."

Tolan smiled. Vicki picked up the locust by one of its legs and held it upside down. The body was shaped like a miniature horse armed for war, but where a mane should have been was long, flowing hair. On its back were wings. Vicki flipped the locust over and saw a human face, but the front teeth were like a lion's.

Lenore trembled. "Don't let it hurt my baby."

"Keep the door closed," Vicki said through clenched teeth. "If this thing gets upstairs it'll sting all of you."

"Put it under the door before it comes to," Shelly said.

Vicki dropped the locust and Shelly kicked it against the wooden door, then mashed its body into the mud.

"Another one's getting in!" Darrion shouted.

Before Vicki could react, a locust skittered by and flew toward the crib. Its wings twitched furiously with a metallic clicking as it rose toward Tolan. The child reached for it and laughed.

"Apollyon," the locust wailed.

Vicki raced for the crib, but the locust disappeared over the edge. Tolan squealed. The locust flew at the child's face, its teeth bared. But it stopped each time, unable to get closer than a few inches from Tolan. The locust darted up, turned to attack, but stopped in midair. Venom sloshed in its tail as it screamed in its high-pitched voice, "Apollyon!" Tolan stared at the locust, then looked at Vicki.

Lenore shrieked, eyeing the door above. "Don't let it get my baby!"

Vicki swung at the locust, but the beast darted behind the crib.

"Get back upstairs, Lenore!" Vicki said.

"We're not letting her back up here!" Melinda shouted. "She won't keep the door closed."

Shelly and Darrion tromped on the floor to keep other locusts out. Vicki helped Lenore up, but the woman fell back, horror on her face.

Vicki turned and saw the locust, its mouth dripping with venom, heading straight for them.

Judd Thompson, Jr. was somehow calm in the middle of so much chaos. Their plane sat on a runway in Jerusalem, trapped by thousands of swarming demons.

The pilot scowled at Judd. "Why aren't you afraid?"

"They won't attack a believer in Christ," Judd said.

"You're crazy."

"I am not," Judd said. "Let me help."

"I can't let you go out there."

Judd put a hand on the pilot's arm. "Anyone else goes out, they'll get stung. Open the door and those things will swarm. If I can get the gate attached, there's a chance these people can get inside the terminal."

The pilot looked out and studied the locusts. "This section of the terminal is isolated."

"Please," Judd said.

The pilot turned to a flight attendant. "Get the crash ax. We'll cut a hole in the baggage compartment."

"Wait," Judd said. "Those things will get through the hole you make."

Something skittered above them. A high-pitched sound followed. "Abbadon!" a locust proclaimed.

"How are they getting in?" the flight attendant said.

The pilot picked up a phone. "Jim, close the manual override to the outflow valve. Now!"

Judd heard locusts scampering overhead. "How thick is that tubing?"

"It's plastic and thick enough," the pilot said. "They can't chew through." He clicked on the intercom. "Ladies and gentlemen, please be seated. There's no way the bugs can get into the cabin. Please stay calm as we work on getting you out of here safely. A young man has offered to help, so clear the aisles and stay in your seats."

Applause greeted Judd as he stepped into the aisle and followed the pilot. The man lifted the edge of the carpet and pulled a yellow tab. The carpet tore along a seam, revealing a small door.

"This leads to a compartment under the plane," he said, grabbing a ring in the floor. "It's tight, but you'll fit."

"The locusts will come in when you open it," Judd said.

The pilot twisted the ring and turned a bolt on the hatch door. "Not if you do it right. It's an access bay. You get inside and we seal the top. Open another door at the bottom and you're outside. No way they can get in."

The pilot showed Judd how to move the jetway into position once he was outside the plane, then opened the hatch. "I hope you're right about them not attacking you."

Judd wriggled to the bottom and found a latch with a weird handle and a button. He pressed and turned it, bracing himself as the hatch opened. Locusts flew into the hole, but

Judd kicked at them. Finally, he let go and dropped to the ground.

Judd felt both relief and horror. The fresh air felt good, but the locusts sickened him. The plane's wings were full of the horrid creatures scratching and biting at the fuselage. Some hovered near the windows, shrieking as they tried to get at the passengers.

White fluid dripped from a burned-out engine. Somehow, the locusts had shattered a rotor and had flown right through the engine. If those locusts had survived, there was no way to kill the beasts.

※

Lionel Washington stood at a window in the terminal. He had lived through an earthquake and the other judgments sent by God, but nothing compared with this.

Sam Goldberg stood beside him, looking equally shocked. Lionel, Sam, and Judd had planned to return to Illinois, but now the world had turned upside down.

"My father," Sam said. "What happens when he is stung?"

Lionel pointed to an airline worker writhing in pain on the runway. "He'll hurt so bad he'll want to kill himself. But he won't be able to."

Sam groaned. "If only he'd listened."

A woman ran screaming through the waiting area and beat on the glass doors. A security guard ran toward her. "You can't go through there, ma'am! It's for your own safety."

"My daughter's in there!"

Lionel saw locusts were on the other side of the glass swooping and attacking as people ran from side to side. Some people cowered in corners. A few tried to hide near pay phones. Others ran for rest rooms and locked themselves inside.

Lionel felt helpless. The only hope for these people was the truth, but they were too frightened to listen.

Sam tugged on Lionel's arm and pointed toward the runway. "Look at that!"

Lionel gasped when Judd crawled out from under the plane and moved toward the terminal. He disappeared beneath the jetway in a swirl of angry locusts.

"We have to help!" Lionel said.

Mark was elated that his new friend, Carl Meninger, had believed the message and was now a follower of Christ. The locusts seemed to know he had stolen a victim.

Mark fired up the motorcycle and the two

rode away. He slowed to a crawl because of all the locusts buzzing around them. "We get hit with one of those and we're dead."

After a few miles Mark pulled to the side of the road. "I can't drive in this. We'll have to wait until they thin out."

He pushed the motorcycle through a grove of trees and into a clearing. The locusts buzzed through the trees looking for more victims. Mark found a spot in the shade and took out food and drinks from his knapsack.

"You saved my life," Carl said. "That's twice somebody from your family has done that."

Mark smiled. "Getting stung hurts, but you wouldn't have died."

Carl took a drink and sat back against the tree. "I have a confession. I said I wanted to meet because of your cousin John. But that's only one reason I came up here. I don't think you're going to like the second."

※

Vicki had dropped her wood plank when she helped Lenore up. Now, with a locust bearing down on them, she swung and smacked it with her hand. Vicki recoiled in pain, like she had hit a metal baseball. Her hand throbbed and swelled.

The locust hurtled backward and hit the

wall. It shook its head, sputtered, then resumed the attack.

"Another one's getting through!" Darrion yelled.

Tolan sat up in his crib and cried for his mother. Vicki joined hands with Shelly and Darrion and they surrounded Lenore, huddling close as three locusts circled menacingly.

"Pray!" Vicki said. "Hurry!"

"God, protect Tolan's mom from these things. Don't let her get stung."

A locust swooped in, brushing Vicki's hair. "In the name of Jesus," Vicki said, "keep them away. God, protect her like you protected your friends in the boat."

"Apollyon!" a demon hissed.

The girls moved closer together, arms linked, heads touching as they stood against the locusts.

"Jesus is King and Lord," Darrion shouted.

"Apollyon!" the demons called out.

"Jesus!" Darrion screamed back. "Jesus is the Christ, the Messiah, the Lamb of God! Get out of here!"

Two locusts hovered over Tolan's crib but moved no closer to him. They clicked their wings and joined the other in midair.

"Let's face them," Vicki said, arms still clasped with Shelly and Darrion.

The hovering locusts looked straight at Vicki. She summoned her courage and looked into their ugly faces, tongues sticking out of gnashing teeth.

"Leave this woman and her baby alone," Vicki said, her teeth clenched. "In the name of Jesus, I command you!"

Over and over they repeated the name of the chief demon, "Apollyon!"

"Jesus has authority!" Shelly said.

"Jesus is the Mighty God," Darrion said.

The locusts seemed to look at each other while Lenore whimpered, her hands covering her head.

Suddenly, Charlie opened the door above and peeked into the room. Vicki yelled, but before the boy could close the door, the three locusts darted up and through the crack. Melinda and Charlie screamed.

Vicki locked the door from the inside. Darrion snatched Tolan from the crib and brought him to Lenore. The woman grabbed for him and he hugged her neck tight.

"I've never seen anything like that," Lenore said. "They were awful."

"And more are trying to get in," Shelly said.

Panting, Lenore scanned the room.

"Settle down," Vicki said, kneeling before

her. "This ought to show you what we're saying is true."

Lenore tried to catch her breath. "I know . . . you kids are religious . . . but I don't know what to do. . . ."

"Jesus is God," Vicki said, pulling Lenore's face toward her. "Do you want to know him?"

Lenore nodded.

"Tell him."

Lenore trembled and bowed her head, her face in her hands. "God, I need you. I know I've done bad things and I'm sorry. Forgive me. I know you're real, and you mean what you say in the Bible. I believe you died for me and that you're coming back after all this is over. So come into my life and make me a new person."

Shelly and Darrion knelt beside Vicki and the woman. When Lenore took her hands away from her face, Vicki saw, forming on Lenore's forehead, the mark of the believer.

TWO

The Spy

JUDD moved past the screaming ground crew and carefully followed the pilot's instructions. He positioned the jetway and picked up a phone.

"These people are going crazy," the pilot said. "We need to get off now."

"Too many of these things buzzing around," Judd said. "Let me clear them out."

"Hurry."

Judd found a fire extinguisher, and to his surprise, the locusts flew away from the white spray.

Something pounded behind him. Lionel was at the door. Judd ran toward him and gave him a thumbs-up. Sam Goldberg stood behind Lionel, waving.

"We've kept them out of this end of the terminal so far," Lionel yelled.

Judd nodded. "Get as many fire extinguishers as you can find and meet me back here!"

As Lionel and Sam scampered away, Judd tried to clear the jetway. There was a gap of a few inches between the plane and the jetway. As he turned the hose on the demons, they flew down the ramp and clustered on the plane door. Judd hit them with another blast from the fire extinguisher, then maneuvered the jetway as tight against the plane as he could.

"We're almost ready," Judd phoned the pilot. "Don't leave the door open long. Let the passengers out about ten at a time. Do you have a fire extinguisher?"

"Yes."

"When I bang on the door, open it and shoot the extinguisher as the passengers get out. Tell them not to stop running until they get to the terminal."

"Got it."

"On my signal," Judd said.

He ran toward the terminal where Lionel and Sam waited with several fire extinguishers. Lionel opened the door and Judd jumped in quickly.

"Wait here for the passengers," Judd told

Sam. "If you see locusts, don't open the door.
We can't let those things in here."

"Man, we're fighting a losing battle,"
Lionel said, grabbing fire extinguishers
and following Judd. They blasted several
locusts that had flown in while Judd was
gone.

"Stand there," Judd said, "and when I
knock on the door, blast your extinguisher
around the hole. If I'm right, those things
will head straight for these people."

Judd rammed his extinguisher into the plane
door twice. It opened a few seconds later as
Judd and Lionel sprayed around the opening.

"Go! Go!" the pilot screamed.

A dozen people darted through the
spray, whimpering and screaming. "Keep
running!" Judd yelled. When the final
person was through, Judd rammed the
door closed and ran backward, calling
Lionel to follow. They sprayed the extinguishers in the air, hoping no locusts
would follow.

The group reached the terminal and
collapsed on chairs, coughing and sputtering.

"So far so good," Lionel said. "Let's get the
next group."

Judd went through the same routine, but
this time more than a dozen streamed out of

the plane. People shoved through, ignoring the pilot's instructions.

Lionel's extinguisher emptied first. As he reached for another, a wave of locusts poured through the opening between the plane and the jetway. A few flew into the plane. Passengers screamed and ran toward the back, scrambling to get away.

Judd backed up, his extinguisher pointed toward the ceiling. He ran past the last few people scrambling toward the terminal door. "Close it now!" Judd yelled to Sam.

When the last person was through, Sam slammed the door shut. Judd and Lionel raced down the jetway and found the plane door open. Judd rushed in first. What he saw would stay with him the rest of his life. People lay on top of each other in the aisle, writhing in pain. Locusts flew at people's heads and arms as they flailed to keep the beasts away. One woman toward the back knocked a demon away with her purse, only to have another fly at her from behind and sting her neck.

Judd opened the cockpit door and found the flight crew slumped over and moaning. The normally calm and collected flight attendant was hysterical. She had been stung on the arm and pushed through the sea of bodies screaming for the first-aid kit.

"What do we do now?" Lionel said.
Judd shook his head.

❋

Vicki ignored the pain in her hand and helped Shelly and Darrion plug the hole by the door. Lenore and Tolan huddled in the corner.

Vicki took the piece of wood and the baby's blanket and opened the door to the room above them. The locusts clicked and buzzed around. Melinda sat on the floor in the middle of the room and Charlie cowered in the corner. Vicki stunned the three locusts and wrapped them in the blanket. She called for Conrad. "I'm holding three trapped demons, can you open the door?"

The locusts inside the blanket were awake now and trying frantically to bite through. Finally, Conrad opened the door, grabbed the bundle, and threw it in the next room.

"Thanks," Vicki said. "Get a couple of beds ready."

"What happened to your hand?" Conrad said.

Vicki waved him off. She closed the door and ran back downstairs. She rolled Melinda over and found she had been stung on the leg. Vicki tried to make her comfortable, then moved to Charlie.

Charlie scooted back into the shadows when Vicki came close. "Are those things coming after me again?"

"It's OK," Vicki said, "they're gone now."

Charlie looked around the room. He still didn't have the mark of the believer, but he wasn't in pain either. "I'm sorry about opening the door," he said, "honest. I just wanted to see what was happening. Before I knew it the three of them flew in and I thought they were going to kill us."

"You weren't stung?" Vicki said.

"They tried," Charlie said. "Two went after her and one came for me. It was ready to bite when it just stopped. Couldn't get closer. And it was screaming and stuff was dripping off its teeth."

Vicki tried to make sense of it. The baby and Charlie had escaped the locusts without the mark of the true believer. Melinda and Janie hadn't. And Lenore was clearly a believer now.

"Help me carry Melinda upstairs," Vicki said.

"Sure, if you promise those things won't bite me."

"I think you're OK," Vicki said.

Charlie carried Melinda on his shoulder and put her on a bed near Janie. The two moaned and begged for something to relieve their pain. The strongest medicine Vicki could find was aspirin. The girls gulped them down and tried to sleep, but there was no relief.

As the day wore on, the locusts thinned out and the kids gathered with Lenore and Tolan. Lenore told her story to Conrad and thanked Vicki and the other girls for praying for her. "I don't know what I would have done without the three of you."

Conrad suggested they write a message to Tsion Ben-Judah and ask why the locusts hadn't stung Tolan or Charlie. Vicki nodded. "And ask him how long this is going to last."

✳

Mark studied Carl. Was this guy leading the GC to them by mistake?

Carl broke the silence. He told Mark about meeting John Preston and training him aboard the Global Community ship *Peace-keeper 1*. John had caught on fast and learned most of the equipment in half the time it took most recruits.

"How did you survive the meteor?" Mark said.

Carl held up a hand. "Let me finish. Your cousin talked about his friends back in Illinois, but he didn't tell me anything about the God stuff until the last day."

"When the meteor hit?" Mark said.

Carl nodded. "When he knew we were all sunk, he got me alone and tried to tell me the truth. I wouldn't listen. So he gave me his spot on the sub."

"What? John could have survived?"

"The captain drew names. He called John's, but John gave up his seat for me." Carl sighed. "Now I finally understand why he did it."

Mark looked at the ground and took a deep breath. He had tried to imagine what John's last hours were like.

"He gave me this as I was getting into the sub," Carl said, handing Mark a Bible.

Mark opened it and saw John's handwriting on the inside cover. It included an e-mail address for Mark and *John 15:12-13. I hope you discover the truth, Carl. God bless you on your journey. John.*

"I could never figure out what those numbers meant after his name," Carl said. "Is that some kind of secret code?"

Mark smiled. "It's a Bible reference." He flipped the pages to the New Testament Gospel of John. His voice caught as he read the words to Carl. "This is something Jesus said to his followers. 'I command you to love each other in the same way that I love you.

And here is how to measure it—the greatest love is shown when people lay down their lives for their friends.' "

Carl grabbed a handful of grass and threw it into the wind. He scratched his chin. "That's what John did. Gave his life for me."

They sat in silence. Finally Mark said, "Can you tell me anything else about him?"

"We kept our sub's monitor on the ship's frequency. John must have barricaded himself inside the command center and preached to everybody on deck. It sounded like the captain was really ticked, the way they were pounding on the door. The sub's skipper made me turn it off. We were all pretty much freakin' out."

"That's the last you heard from him?"

"Yeah. I'm sorry. If I'd have refused his offer, he'd be here with you right now."

Mark shook his head. "No, he wouldn't. He'd have found somebody else who didn't know God and given up his seat to them."

Carl nodded. "You're probably right."

"What happened in the sub?"

"We went down as far and as fast as we could go," Carl said. "We were carrying a few civilians we'd rescued from a drug ship. One guy had seen way too many of those movies where the submarine ruptures and everybody dies. It was all we could do to keep them calm and not use up all the oxygen.

"The navigator took us as far away from the splashdown site as he could. We heard the impact and braced. It took a couple of minutes for the wave to reach us, but when it did, it just took control. Even as far down as we were, it picked up that sub like a toy and brought us to the surface in seconds."

"You could've died," Mark said.

"A lot did," Carl said. "All but two of the civilians. Six of us from the *Peacekeeper 1* made it out alive. I was in the hospital for a long time. That's why I didn't get in touch with you sooner."

"Why didn't we hear anything from the media about this?" Mark said. "It should have been big news."

"The GC kept it quiet," Carl said.

"Must have been hairy inside that sub."

Carl took a breath. "I'll never forget it. People screaming. Everybody yelling, asking God to save them."

"Why'd you wait until now to believe what John told you?"

"That's what you're not going to like," Carl said. "When I finally woke up in the hospital, a GC security guy was there asking questions. I told him everything. I told him about John, about what he'd said about God—"

"That was stupid!"

"I know that now. I thought I was doing the right thing."

Mark stood. "John saved your life and you wanted to sell us out?"

"They asked me to get as much information as I could over the Internet," Carl said. "I didn't know what to do. They figured anybody mixed up with somebody like John had to be another religious fanatic. So I wrote you."

"And you led them right to me," Mark said. "Conrad warned me not to—"

"That's not why I'm here!" Carl shouted. "When I was trying to get in touch with you, I started reading some of the stuff John gave me. But I got stuck and I wanted to ask you some questions."

"And report to your friends in the GC!"

"I'm not going to do that. I know the truth now and you helped me see it. But you have to know something else."

"What?"

"The GC is gearing up, getting information on people like you—I mean, like us, all around the country. Around the world."

"We've known for a long time that the GC doesn't like followers of Tsion Ben-Judah—"

"But they're getting organized," Carl said.

"The GC has names and addresses of people who visit the rabbi's Web site. They haven't acted yet, but they're going to."

"What are you saying?"

"Take me to your hideout and teach me everything you can," Carl said. "I want to learn about God. Then I want to go out and warn those people before it's too late."

THREE

The Warning

JUDD backed out of the plane and walked up the jetway with Lionel. Everyone in the plane had been stung and were wailing and moaning.

The sight inside the terminal wasn't much better. Locusts had burrowed through ceiling tiles and attacked people at will. A woman carrying a baby ran screaming. The locusts attacked her but left the baby alone.

A man stood in the corner holding a bottle of water. When the demons flew at him, he threw the bottle toward them. As water poured onto the floor, it turned bright red.

"Blood!" Lionel said as the demons hissed even louder and stung the man.

"We've done all we can here," Judd said. He found a stairwell and led Lionel and Sam outside. Suffering people filled the roadway.

Some had their windows rolled down when the locusts attacked. They were slumped behind steering wheels. Others had crashed trying to avoid the beasts and were attacked when they got out.

Judd tried to flag down a taxi, but even those sitting still wouldn't open their doors in fear of the locusts.

"Where are we going?" Sam said.

"No way we'll get a flight out," Judd said. "Let's head to Jamal's place."

Lionel shook his head. "I don't think he'll be too happy—"

"He'll be thrilled when I tell him about Africa." Judd briefly explained how he and Mr. Stein had discovered a remote tribe in the country of Mali. When Mr. Stein had spoken, the village had understood every word. "He stayed to talk to more tribes."

"That's a great story," Lionel said, "but Jamal was really ticked off after what happened with you and Nada. He seemed pretty glad to get rid of us."

"Let's just head back to Jerusalem and figure it out from there," Judd said.

While Judd and Lionel talked, Sam wandered into the traffic. A few moments later he called for them. "This man's a believer and says he can take us as far as the Old City," Sam said.

The three hopped in and Judd told them
more about what happened in Africa. They
were surprised at how God had cared for the
details of their trip and prepared the hearts of
the tribe.

The driver turned to Judd. "I was here to
pick up a friend who is also a believer. His
plane was diverted to Tel Aviv, but I'm sure
things won't be any better there."

As they neared the Old City of Jerusalem,
the driver offered to take them wherever they
wanted. "My friend will wait."

"Thank you," Judd said. "We can walk."

"God bless you," the driver said.

They passed a hospital where hundreds
stood outside. Locusts buzzed around them,
attacking people on the street and fluttering
near doorways and windows, hoping to sting
more victims. One man draped a heavy blanket over himself and crawled across the
street, but the locusts finally flew inside and
stung him.

Judd realized they were close to the
Wailing Wall and motioned Lionel and
Sam forward. As they neared the site, Eli
and Moishe yelled their message to a small
crowd of believers who lay flat on the
ground. Unmanned cameras and micro-
phones recorded the event.

"You rant and rave against God for the terrible plague that has befallen you!" Eli said. "Though you will be the last, you were not the first generation who forced God's loving hand to act in discipline.

"Listen to these words from the ancient of days, the Lord God of Israel: I also withheld the rain from you, when there were still three months to the harvest. I made it rain on one city; I withheld rain from another city. One part was rained upon, and where it did not rain the part withered.

"So two or three cities wandered to another city to drink water, but they were not satisfied; yet you have not returned to me."

Eli spoke again. "I blasted you with blight and mildew. When your gardens . . . increased, the locust devoured them; yet you have not returned to me. I sent among you a plague after the manner of Egypt; your young men I killed with a sword . . . yet you have not returned to me."

Judd moved closer and noticed several people who had been stung by locusts. They moaned and cried softly as the witnesses continued.

"Forgive me," one man said. "I didn't listen and I'm paying the price."

Though his pain continued, the man immediately received the mark of the true believer.

Eli continued. "Prepare to meet your God, O Israel! For behold, he who forms the mountains, and creates the wind, who declares to man what his thought is, and makes the morning darkness, who treads the high places of the earth; the Lord God of hosts is his name.

"Thus says the Lord to the house of Israel: Seek me and live . . . Hate evil, love good; establish justice in the gate. It may be that the Lord God of hosts will be gracious to the remnant of Joseph.

"Though you offer me burnt offerings and your meat offerings, I will not accept them, nor will I regard your fattened peace offerings. Take away from me the noise of your songs, for I will not hear the melody of your stringed instruments.

"But let justice run down like water, and righteousness like a mighty stream."

Later that day, Vicki called a meeting. She read an e-mail message from Tsion Ben-Judah. When the kids were seated, she began.

> *"Dear Friends of the Young Tribulation Force,*
>   *"Thank you for telling me of your*

encounter with the locusts predicted in Revelation 9. As you know, these creatures will not harm grass or plants or trees, but will attack people who do not have the seal of God on their foreheads.

"As for the baby, Tolan, he is protected by the same love God had for the infants taken in the Rapture. God would not allow these beasts to plague a little child like this. His love and mercy continues, even in these dark times.

"I rejoice that because of your prayers, Lenore has been spared and has actually believed in the message of the gospel. This is the first time I have heard the locusts were hindered by the prayers of believers. I pray Lenore will learn much of God's word through you."

Vicki paused and looked at Charlie. He sat on the edge of his seat, tapping his foot.

"Does it say somethin' about me?" Charlie said.

Vicki nodded.

"Keep praying for Charlie. I don't know why the locusts didn't attack him, but we have to believe that God's love is at work in his life just as it is in Tolan's."

Charlie smiled.

"Scripture indicates the locusts will seek out victims for the next five months. From my reading, I believe the effects of the sting will last five months as well. Therefore, unbelievers will be secluded or suffering for many months.

"This is a great opportunity for us. I believe we must use this time to move about and network with other believers for the terrible time that is to come in the future.

"I continue to receive incredible response to my Web site. Many teenagers have written with questions and I am unable to respond personally to them. Judd told me of his trip to Israel and I know he cannot answer as many as he would like. Would any of you be able to respond to these questions?

"Thank you for your service to the King of kings and Lord of lords. May God bless you as you tell others about his love.

"Sincerely in the love of Christ,
"Tsion Ben-Judah."

Conrad held up a hand. "Why can't we have a Web site? We could post the most-asked questions and the answers and call it theunderground-online.com.

"We could have a link to Dr. Ben-Judah's Web site," Darrion said.

Vicki said, "Wouldn't that put us in more danger from the Global Community? Supreme What's-His-Face says anybody who visits the Ben-Judah Web site will be fined and imprisoned."

Conrad laughed. "If that's true, they're going to have to build a lot more prisons. I think he's just trying to scare people."

"A lot of kids are asking questions," Shelly said. "We could reach millions this way."

Vicki weighed the risks. It seemed like God was giving them more opportunities every day, even from this remote place.

"OK," Vicki said, "start working on it. But I want to talk about it with Mark when he gets back."

Lenore approached Vicki after the meeting and said she was excited to start learning more about the Bible. "I want to do anything I can for you kids. Cook. Clean. I can even give some medical help if you need it."

"Medical?" Vicki said.

"I was studying to be a nurse just before I got married," Lenore said. "I was a little more than a year away from graduation when Tolan was born."

Vicki unrolled the bandage from her hand. She winced when Lenore held her hand.

"It doesn't look broken, but you've got a

bad bruise there. Better get something cold on it fast."

Vicki nodded and led Lenore upstairs to see what she could do for Janie and Melinda.

❋

Mark didn't know whether he could trust Carl. Mark knew the boy was sincere about his faith. That was clear as the mark on his forehead.

"The GC knows about Dr. Ben-Judah, but they can't find him," Carl said. "There's even a reward for any GC officer that finds information about where he's located."

"A bounty?" Mark said.

Carl nodded. "And there are other rewards for people who bring in rebels—people like us. It's very secret, but the operation is new."

"How much would they offer for someone like you?" Mark said.

"I don't even want to think about it," Carl said. "They found one group in South Carolina just before I left. They were set to move in on them."

Mark looked at the sky. The locusts had moved north to more populated areas. The two got back on the motorcycle and drove

away slowly, but Mark still had questions.
Should he take Carl to the hideout?

Judd, Lionel, and Sam walked through the
Old City streets. From windows and doors
came the screams of people who had been
stung by the locusts. The sound of the
winged creatures was like a thundering herd
of horses.

"Will anybody not get stung?" Sam said.

"Everybody without the mark is fair
game," Judd said. "Why?"

"I'm thinking of my father," Sam said. "If
he avoids these things, perhaps he'll listen."

Judd convinced them to go to Jamal's
house and they backtracked to the right
street. When they turned the corner and saw
the apartment building, Judd gasped. Three
Global Community squad cars were in front
of the building, lights flashing.

Judd, Lionel, and Sam raced to the front
entrance and buzzed. Several uniformed officers were on the floor inside, writhing in
pain. A woman who had been stung
managed to open the door for them.

"What are they doing here?" Judd asked,
pointing toward the officers, but the woman
was in too much pain to answer.

Judd ran toward the elevator. He stopped in his tracks when an old man cackled.

"The GC's going to get them!" the man said, talking through a crack in the door. "I told the GC what the people upstairs were teaching." The man squinted at Lionel. "*You're* one of them too! I saw you down here speaking against the potentate."

A locust buzzed nearby and the man slammed the door. Judd ran to the elevator. The man behind the door yelled, "They're taking them away! I hope they get the whole group!"

"Jamal and his family!" Lionel said.

"I hope we're not too late," Sam said as he stepped into the elevator. A locust flew inside, then tried to get out, but the elevator door clanged shut. The locust buzzed around the lights above and finally came to rest on the floor, panting. Judd took off his shirt and trapped the creature.

"What are you doing?" Sam said.

"We may need him," Judd said.

When the elevator reached the twelfth floor, the three ran down the hall. They took the stairs two at a time and reached Jamal's door. Judd smacked the demon locust and tried to keep it quiet, but the thing kept yelling a muffled, "Abbadon!"

Judd listened closely at the door. Someone was yelling questions at Jamal and his family.

"The fire escape leads to our room," Lionel said.

Quickly they took the stairs to the roof and climbed down the fire escape. Judd opened the window easily and climbed inside. Lionel and Sam followed, closing the window before any locusts could get inside.

Lionel put the trapped locust under a mattress and sat on it. Judd put a finger to his lips and opened the door slightly. Jamal, his wife, and Nada sat with their backs to Judd, their hands cuffed behind them. The GC officer paced in front of them, barking questions Jamal didn't answer.

"I know this guy," Judd whispered to Sam and Lionel. "He was with your dad when they questioned me."

"Deputy Commander Woodruff," Sam said. "He's pretty tough."

Judd listened closely. Two other GC officers were in the apartment.

"We know you have illegally housed people who are against the Global Community," Woodruff said. "We know from inside sources that you have spoken out against Potentate Carpathia and the Supreme Pontiff."

"We have only spoken the truth," Jamal muttered.

Deputy Commander Woodruff leaned close. "Then tell us the truth about where Rabbi Ben-Judah is hiding."

As Judd listened, he noticed something familiar about Woodruff's voice. Judd was sure he had met the man before the questioning. *But where?*

Jamal and the others remained silent. The deputy commander sighed and walked across the room. Another officer spoke and called attention to the locusts outside.

"Since you know so much about the future, you must know a way we can avoid these ghastly creatures."

"*I* do," Nada said.

"Tell me."

Nada sat straight in her chair. "Believe on the Lord Jesus Christ and you will be saved."

Deputy Commander Woodruff slapped her. Jamal struggled to get up, but the man pushed him back, sending his chair to the floor. Jamal's arms were pinned behind him. He screamed in pain and opened his eyes, looking directly at Judd.

Judd put a finger to his lips.

"Shut up!" Woodruff said.

Suddenly, Judd remembered where he had heard Woodruff's voice. A chill went up his spine. Judd knew exactly what he had to do.

FOUR

The Sting

Judd motioned to Lionel for the locust. Lionel slid off the bed and pulled the shirt from beneath the mattress. The locust screeched and tried to click its wings. Judd held it tightly and listened as Deputy Commander Woodruff told the two GC officers to check the first floor and see if the locusts were still there.

"Good thing we didn't stay in the hall," Lionel whispered.

Judd told Lionel and Sam to stay out of sight from the door. If they needed to run, he'd give the signal.

Woodruff approached Jamal and hovered over him. "Tell us what you know about Ben-Judah and we will free you. Keep playing games and I'll be forced to act. First against your wife, then your daughter."

Judd fumed. When Woodruff yelled, Judd pieced the clues together about the man. Judd had vowed revenge against him.

"You can't treat us like this," Jamal protested. "The Global Community would not allow—"

"Do you see any witnesses?" the deputy commander said. "Either you tell me what I want to know or—"

Judd opened the door. "There *are* witnesses. Just like there were witnesses when you killed those two in Tel Aviv."

Woodruff turned, surprised. "What are you talking about? Who are you?" Woodruff yelled for the other officers.

Judd took a step into the room. "I was on the phone when you killed my friends, Taylor and Hasina. You said they resisted arrest and you were forced to kill them. You lied."

"Judd, get out of here!" Nada yelled.

"Judd?" Woodruff said, reaching for his gun. "That wasn't the name you gave at the station."

Judd stood his ground. "I was on the other end of the phone when you killed my friends. I said you wouldn't get away with it, and you won't."

"I should have dealt with you while I had the chance," Woodruff said. "If it hadn't been for Goldberg and the people at headquarters, you'd still be locked up."

"I'm going to give you the chance you never gave my friends," Judd said. "Walk out of here and leave these people alone."

Woodruff shook his head and moved a step toward Judd. "You're in no position to bargain."

Judd held up the shirt. "Abbadon," the locust said.

"This is the next judgment from God," Judd said. "These locusts will sting those who don't believe and they'll feel incredible pain. You'll want to die, but you won't be able to."

Woodruff scoffed and held up his gun. "You can't scare me with your little animal."

"You can't kill it," Judd said.

The elevator doors opened downstairs. Footsteps approached quickly.

Woodruff leveled the gun at Judd. "Now you'll see what a mistake you made coming here."

Judd opened the shirt and the locust skittered into the air, disoriented. It looked at Jamal and his family, then spotted Deputy Commander Woodruff. "Abbadon," it screamed, its teeth dripping venom.

Woodruff jumped back, terror on his face. The locust darted toward the ceiling. Woodruff shot and missed.

Judd ran for the front door and locked it. The other officers shouted outside.

Judd turned and the locust dived for Woodruff. The man fired wildly and missed again, the bullet lodging in a wall. Then the locust was on him, biting his forehead.

"Deputy Commander!" an officer screamed outside. "What's wrong?"

Woodruff swatted at the locust but it was too late. The venom immediately entered the man's bloodstream. He thrashed and yelled in pain. His gun rattled to the floor.

Judd stepped over Jamal and his family and knelt beside Woodruff. The locust flew toward the front door.

"Get it off me!" Woodruff screamed, swatting at the locust that wasn't there.

Judd grabbed keys from the man's belt and quickly unlocked the handcuffs. The officers outside kicked at the door. Lionel opened the window and a few more locusts flew inside.

"I wouldn't come in here if I were you," Jamal shouted. "There is a gang of locusts waiting for you."

The pounding stopped. The men yelled for their leader, but he was still thrashing and moaning on the floor. Lionel and Sam helped Jamal's wife and Nada to their feet. Sam grabbed the gun and stuffed it under the mattress in the next room.

"We have to hurry," Judd said to Jamal.

One by one they climbed onto the fire

escape. Judd was the last one out the window. As he crawled outside, the front door splintered. Then came the frightened cries of men who were now face-to-face with evil.

※

Vicki and Lenore tried to help Melinda and Janie but nothing worked. The girls were just as miserable as when they were first stung.

"We have to make them comfortable and leave it at that," Lenore whispered as she and Vicki left the bedroom.

The other kids complained about the moaning and crying upstairs. "This is going to get spooky if it keeps up through the night," Darrion said.

As evening approached, the kids gathered to eat and talk about what had happened. Everyone had questions about the locusts and what was ahead. Charlie drank in every word. Conrad found an Internet news outlet and turned it up so everyone could hear. The news anchor had locked himself inside the studio to keep the locusts out.

"We can't estimate the millions of people who have been stung," the anchor said, "but reports are flooding in from throughout the world. All modes of transportation have come to a standstill. Hospitals are jammed with patients, but in many there is no one to treat the wounded. Doctors and nurses have been stung as well."

The anchor spoke by phone with a scientist in Philadelphia who had miraculously escaped the locusts.

"These creatures seem to be a hybrid," the scientist said, "between a horse, a lion, a human being, and an insect. I've looked at the venom closely and this isn't like any other I've ever seen. It attacks the central nervous system and causes severe pain. The good news is, the sting is not fatal. The bad news is, there seems to be no letup to the pain."

The anchor continued. "That diagnosis seems to be true. With all the reports of locust attacks, we still haven't been notified of anyone dying because of an attack."

"I wonder if Nicolae Carpathia will get stung," Shelly said.

"The locusts are probably too scared to go near the guy," Conrad said.

※

Instead of heading to the schoolhouse, Mark took Carl toward the suburbs of Chicago. They made it to Z's gas station by nightfall and Z's father led them downstairs.

While Carl grabbed something to eat,

Mark explained why he was there. Z listened and scratched his neck. "If he's got the mark and the locusts haven't stung him, that's proof he's one of us."

"I'm scared to take him back to the hideout," Mark said. "He could lead the GC to us."

Z nodded. "I understand. He could lead them here, too, did you think of that? But where else is he going to get the kind of teaching you guys can give him?"

Z took Mark to his office and showed him how much money he had made from the coins the kids had found. "I've already sold almost half of them." Z pointed to a figure on the screen.

"Incredible!"

"With that money, plus what I get for the other half, we should be able to buy lots of food and supplies to send to believers around the country."

"How are you going to ship the stuff?" Mark said.

"A couple of pilots I know will take care of the flights overseas," Z said, "and I've already got drivers lined up for the States and Canada. I think you know one of them."

"Who?"

"Guy named Pete."

"The biker?" Mark said.

"Yeah. He's supposed to be coming here with a rig from down south. He's got an amazin' story."

"I can't wait to hear it," Mark said.

※

Judd and the others crammed into Jamal's car and drove away. The GC squad cars were still in front of the building, their lights swirling.

Judd told them what had happened at the airport. Jamal wanted to hear about Mr. Stein and their trip to Africa, but Judd said he would tell them later.

"We will not be able to return to our home," Jamal said. "We are fugitives."

"What about our things?" Jamal's wife said.

Jamal shook his head.

Lionel told them about the man downstairs who said he contacted the GC.

"We knew it was dangerous trying to help others in the building," Jamal said. "A few of them have believed our message. For that I am grateful."

Locusts buzzed the streets. People who had been stung moaned and screamed along the sidewalk. They passed a few cars. Everyone who hadn't been stung was staying inside.

"Look out!" Jamal's wife shouted as they drove through an intersection.

A woman stepped in front of the car. Jamal swerved, but it was too late. They hit the woman at full speed, smashing the right headlight. The woman flew through the air and landed with a sickening thud on the pavement. Judd and Nada ran to help.

Judd felt the woman's neck for a pulse. "She's still alive!"

The woman groaned and rocked her head.

"Why did you do that?" Nada asked.

"I don't want to live!" the woman screamed. "Please, I can't take the pain."

Jamal phoned an ambulance, but there was no answer. They helped the woman to a nearby bench. When another car came near, she leaped from her seat and ran into the road.

Jamal brought Judd and Nada back to the car. "She won't die. But there's nothing we can do for her now."

They drove to the home of Yitzhak Weizmann, the man who had helped Judd, Lionel, and Mr. Stein find a place to stay when they first arrived in Jerusalem. Yitzhak welcomed them with food and listened to their story. "Don't worry. You will stay here."

Jamal motioned for Judd to join him in

the living room as everyone pulled out blankets and pillows for the night.

"I promise I won't be a problem," Judd said.

Jamal looked hard at Judd. "Nada told me everything. I was . . . stern with you. Too hard. I would be grateful if you would accept my apology and my thanks for saving our lives this evening."

Judd smiled. "Apology accepted."

* * *

The last time Mark had seen Pete, he was heading south with some of his gang. The rattle of the 18-wheeler shook Z's gas station. Mark reached to shake hands, but Pete grabbed him in a bear hug and Mark could hardly breathe. Pete was still big, but it looked like he had lost some weight.

Mark and Carl helped Pete unload supplies and stash them deep in Z's hideout. When they finished, Z's father had dinner ready. Mark couldn't remember when he'd had a better meal.

Mark brought them up to date on the kids and introduced Carl. Pete was surprised that Judd and Lionel were in Israel, but he was glad Mr. Stein had been able to attend the Meeting of the Witnesses. Pete asked about

Vicki and the schoolhouse. Mark told him about Taylor Graham's death.

Pete hung his head. "I hoped Taylor would become one of us."

"My cousin John also died," Mark said.

Carl explained what had happened.

Tears came to Pete's eyes as he listened. "I'm glad you came to the truth, son."

Z asked about the condition of the roads.

"It's pretty rough in places," Pete said. "With a cycle it's a breeze, but with the 18-wheeler you have to take it slow."

"Where you going next?" Mark said.

"I head to Florida tomorrow. We hooked up with a believer who can get us food that won't spoil. I'll take it north and put it in a warehouse, then head back this way."

"How did you get into trucking?" Mark said.

"I've met a lot of people over the years," Pete said. "Sometime ago I was through Alabama and Mississippi and hooked up with some good friends. I left to find them and tell them the truth."

"What happened?"

Pete smiled and took another bite of pie. "I had hoped everybody I talked with would become a believer. Didn't happen. A few believed, though. We even started a church at one of the truck stops."

"How'd you get the truck?" Mark asked.

"An older guy I know got hurt in the earthquake. Said he wanted me to drive his rig. I told him I wasn't interested, but he wouldn't take no for an answer. Said he thought God wanted me to have it."

"Another driver down south told me about Pete," Z said. "We talked and he agreed to come on board."

"This is the perfect time to store provisions," Pete said. "With all the locusts attacking people, it's like we're the only ones on the road. The GC won't be able to keep track of us."

Carl told them about the GC plans to find believers throughout the country. "I'm not going back to active duty. I have to warn those people."

Pete scratched his chin and looked at Carl. "You might want to rethink that. I don't pretend to know everything, but maybe God wants you to stay on the inside. That could be a big help."

"But dangerous," Mark said. "If they catch you—"

"I don't care about that," Carl said. "I wanted to get more teaching and make sure we warn as many as we can."

"I'll take you to the schoolhouse tomorrow," Pete said. "You'll get a crash course there and then you can decide."

Carl nodded and stared at his plate. Mark knew whatever Carl decided would be dangerous, but if it meant saving the lives of believers, he was ready.

FIVE

Janie's Pain

THOUGH he was exhausted, Lionel couldn't get to sleep. When he closed his eyes, images of frightened people on the plane flashed in his mind. He saw the locusts, teeth bared, attacking the passengers. He thought of the woman inside the airport terminal and wondered if she had found her daughter. So many needed help.

Judd and Sam slept soundly, which increased Lionel's frustration. He tossed and turned until the wee hours of the morning, then gave up and went to the kitchen for a drink. He found Yitzhak at the kitchen table pecking away at a laptop computer.

"Every morning I thank God for a new day to live and be part of this adventure," Yitzhak whispered. He pulled out a chair for Lionel. "I could very easily be in heaven right now.

The GC could have killed me while I was locked up there, but they didn't. So God must have something for me to do."

Yitzhak turned. "Do you realize we have something other believers have never had?"

"What's that?" Lionel said.

"We know when Jesus will return! Believe me, I wish I had recognized the Messiah, but even though we are going through terrible times, each new judgment from God is a sign that he is real and he keeps his promises."

Yitzhak had logged on to Tsion Ben-Judah's Web site and read it carefully. "Tsion believes, though he admits it's only a guess, that the locusts need bite a person once, and then they move on. I haven't seen one up close yet."

Lionel shook his head in disgust. "I have and it's not a pretty picture."

"I'm glad they're working for God and not against believers."

"What do you mean?" Lionel said.

"If Tsion is right that these are demons, these creatures must be going crazy. They hate believers. They must want to kill us, but they are under instructions from God to torture only unbelievers."

"What Satan means for evil, God is using for good."

"Exactly," Yitzhak said.

Lionel looked out the window. Yellow light signaled another beautiful sunrise. But with the beauty came the racket of the locusts searching for new victims. "I don't know if I can take five months of that noise."

"Look at this," Yitzhak said, pulling up the latest report from the 144,000 witnesses. Like Mr. Stein, they were reaching remote tribal groups that understood the message in their own language. Those people were becoming tribulation saints and spreading the message even more.

"I can't wait for Mr. Stein to get back and tell his story," Lionel said.

"That may take months," Yitzhak said. "Transportation is at a standstill."

Tsion wrote that one day the world system would require a mark on every person to buy and sell. Once a person took the mark offered by the Global Community, it would seal the fate of that person for all time, just as the mark of the believer sealed the person as a child of God forever.

I beg of you not to look upon God as mean when we see the intense suffering of the bite victims. This is all part of his master design to turn people to him so he can demonstrate his love. The Scriptures tell us God is ready to pardon, gracious and merciful, slow to anger, and abundant in kindness. How it must pain him to have to resort to such measures to reach those he loves!

It hurts us to see that even those who do receive Christ as a result of this ultimate attention-getter still suffer for the entire five months prescribed in biblical prophecy. And yet I believe we are called to see this as a picture of the sad fact that sin and rebellion have their consequences. There are scars. If a victim receives Christ, God has redeemed him, and he stands perfect in heaven's sight. But the effects of sin linger.

Oh, dear ones, it thrills my heart to get reports from all over the globe that there are likely more Christ followers now than were raptured. Even nations known for only a tiny Christian impact in the past are seeing great numbers come to salvation.

Of course we see that evil is also on the rise. The Scriptures tell us that those who remain rebellious even in light of this awful plague simply love themselves and their sin too much. Much as the world system tries to downplay it, our society has seen catastrophic rises in drug abuse, sexual immorality, murder, theft, demon worship, and idolatry.

Be of good cheer even in the midst of chaos and plague, loved ones. We know from the Bible that the evil demon king of the abyss is living up to his name— Abaddon in Hebrew and Apollyon in Greek, which means Destroyer—in leading the demon locusts on the rampage. But we as the sealed followers of the Lord God need not fear. For as it is written: "He who is in you is greater than he who is in the world. . . . We are of God. He who knows God hears us; he who is not of God does not hear us. By this we know the spirit of truth and the spirit of error."

Always test my teaching against the Bible. Read it every day. New believers— and none of us are old, are we?—learn the value of the discipline of daily reading and study. When we see the ugly creatures that have invaded the earth, it becomes obvious that we too must go to war.

Yitzhak turned the computer screen toward him and read the next paragraphs aloud. Through trembling lips he read:

"Finally, my brethren, with the apostle Paul I urge you to 'be strong in the Lord and in the power of His might. Put on the whole armor of God, that you may be able

to stand against the wiles of the devil. For we do not wrestle against flesh and blood, but against principalities, against powers, against the rulers of the darkness of this age, against spiritual hosts of wickedness in the heavenly places.

" 'Therefore take up the whole armor of God, that you may be able to withstand in the evil day, and having done all, to stand. Stand therefore, having girded your waist with truth, having put on the breastplate of righteousness, and having shod your feet with the preparation of the gospel of peace; above all, taking the shield of faith with which you will be able to quench all the fiery darts of the wicked one.

" 'And take the helmet of salvation, and the sword of the Spirit, which is the word of God; praying always with all prayer and supplication in the Spirit, being watchful to this end with all perseverance and supplication for all the saints—and for me, that utterance may be given to me, that I may open my mouth boldly to make known the mystery of the gospel.'

"Until next we interact through this miracle of technology the Lord has used to build a mighty church against all odds, I remain your servant and his, Tsion Ben-Judah."

"Pray with me," Yitzhak said, bowing his head. "Lord God, I ask your protection on my young friend and his companions. Give them strength to follow your will. Show them the way to go and give them peace."

Lionel went back to his room and thought about what Tsion had written. Though the demons were terrifying and the world was in chaos, God was in control and would be victorious.

The sun peeked over the horizon and sunshine streamed through the window as Lionel put his head on the pillow and fell asleep.

* * *

It had been a long, exhausting day for Vicki. On normal nights the kids would stay up late talking or searching the Internet for the latest news. On this night they went to their rooms quietly and fell into bed.

Vicki jolted awake. Something moved. A locust landed on the covers of her bed. "Apollyon!" the creature said.

Vicki kicked at the covers and the locust flew away. She shuddered and thought about what had happened that day. Earlier, Conrad had played a game with Charlie and Darrion, seeing who could hit the most locusts with a baseball bat. Each took turns swatting at the beasts. Conrad made up rules as he went along. The kids were awarded singles, doubles, and home runs, depending on how far the locusts were hit and how long they were unable to fly.

Charlie hit two locusts with one swing and the kids cheered. Darrion timed a swing perfectly and hit one locust into another. One locust screamed, "Apollyon" just as Conrad whacked it past the tree line. "No," Conrad said, "Apolly-going-going-gone!"

Lenore shook her head and took Tolan inside.

Shelly said the game was gruesome. "You're playing with demons!"

"Maybe we're saving somebody some pain," Conrad said. "If we keep these busy, they can't sting somebody else."

"It's just not right," Shelly said.

"We're just having a little fun," Darrion said.

"Can't you do something?" Shelly said to Vicki.

Vicki shrugged as Shelly went back inside. She finally asked them to stop when Conrad put duct tape on a locust's wing and watched it fly in a circle.

"Where do you think these things will go when they're finished stinging people?" Conrad said.

Now Vicki thought about the question as she lay awake. Maybe they would go back into the hole where the meteor hit. Perhaps they would disappear when God was through with them.

Someone moaned and footsteps sounded on the floor above her. Vicki climbed the stairs. Melinda was alone in the upstairs bedroom, half asleep but still writhing in pain. Janie's bed was empty. A door closed downstairs. Vicki walked quietly to the kitchen and tried the door to the basement. Suddenly, two locusts shot past her screaming, "Apollyon!"

Vicki jumped back and took a deep breath. She wondered when things would get back to normal. But what was *normal* now? People vanishing, earthquakes, meteors, freezing temperatures, and now flying demons. Nothing was like it used to be.

Something spilled in the kitchen and Vicki found Janie kneeling, picking up pills and stuffing them into her mouth.

"No!" Vicki said, grabbing the jar away from her.

"Give it back," Janie said. "I want to take all of them and get this over with."

Vicki shook her head. "It doesn't matter how many you take, you won't die."

Janie slumped to the floor and cried. Vicki put an arm around her, but the girl pushed her away.

"How long will you run from the truth?" Vicki said. "We tried to warn you and you wouldn't believe us."

Janie moaned and reached for more pills. Vicki dragged her from the pantry and closed the door.

"If I believe like you guys, will it take away the pain?" Janie said.

"No. Once you've been stung, you've just got to ride it out. And it might get worse."

"Worse!?!"

"You still have the chance to believe," Vicki said. "God will forgive you."

"I helped that woman and her baby. I put my life on the line for them. What more do I need to do?"

"You still think that doing good things will make you OK with God. That's not how it works."

"I've tried my best," Janie said.

"No. You didn't listen to a thing we've told you about how to connect with God. You've tried to be a good person and do good things so they'd outweigh the dumb stuff you've done."

"What dumb stuff?"

"The drugs and the lying," Vicki said. "You

almost got yourself killed back at the detention center because nobody trusted you."

"Wasn't my fault," Janie whined.

"When are you going to take responsibility for your life? You're the one who's gotten yourself into this mess. Don't blame anyone else."

Janie grabbed her stomach and rolled on the floor. "How can you be so cruel, preaching to me when I'm in so much pain?"

"Because this is the first time you're listening. Maybe getting stung by that locust will be worth it if you finally realize—"

"Nothing is worth this much pain," Janie said. "You don't know what it feels like."

"You're right, I don't. But the pain you're feeling now is nothing compared to the pain of being separated from God forever. Multiply what you're feeling right now by about a million and—"

"Don't try to scare me."

"I'm telling you the truth!" Vicki yelled. She wondered if she had awakened anyone in the house. She paused, then heard Tolan cry in another room. A few minutes later he stopped and apparently went back to sleep.

Vicki looked closely at Janie and was scared. The girl's eyes were hollow and her lips chapped. Her face was white as a sheet.

"If God would do this to me," Janie said, "I don't want to *connect* with him. He doesn't care."

"That's not true," Vicki said. She grabbed a Bible. "God could have wiped out everybody who didn't believe in him. Instead, he's being patient with us."

"How do you figure that?"

Vicki turned to Second Peter. "This was written a long time before the disappearances, but it's still true. It says, 'He does not want anyone to perish, so he is giving more time for everyone to repent.' A little later it says, 'The Lord is waiting so that people have time to be saved.' "

Janie rolled her eyes. "God is stinging us and putting us through earthquakes because he cares? I say that's a weird way of showing it."

"Don't you see?" Vicki said. "This is your only hope."

But no matter how Vicki tried to explain God's love, Janie wouldn't listen. She stood and hobbled toward the stairs. "If you can find anything in there about how to kill yourself, let me know."

Vicki made sure Janie made it to bed before she went to her own room. Melinda awoke a few minutes later and screamed for some medicine to help with the pain.

It's going to be a long five months, Vicki thought.

SIX

Travel Plans

THE next day, Vicki heard a truck and rushed outside. The paralyzing fear that the GC would show up and bust them was gone, but anytime the kids heard a strange noise they knew it could be trouble. She stayed behind a tree and watched.

Vicki couldn't place the driver and the other passenger, but she knew Mark's smile. He jumped out and introduced Carl. Vicki noticed Carl had the mark of the believer.

"And you're not going to believe who I ran into," Mark said. A burly man walked out from behind the truck.

"Pete!" Vicki screamed.

Pete hugged Vicki and the others, then turned to the schoolhouse. "Some place."

"Works for us," Vicki said. "Come inside and catch us up on everything—"

Pete shook his head. "Work first, talk later."

The kids pitched in and unloaded the truck. This was the biggest shipment Z had sent them. They filled the shed and the storage area near the kitchen and moved to the basement. They even lined the underground tunnel with canned food, making sure there was room to get by in case they needed a quick escape.

Pete heard the moans and cries of Melinda and Janie upstairs. Vicki explained the situation and introduced Lenore and Tolan.

The truck was nearly empty when Pete suggested they take a break for lunch. He told the kids what had happened on his trip south. Vicki thought it incredible how God had prepared Pete to give the gospel message to people around the country. Each truck stop was a new opportunity.

While the others ate, Conrad asked Mark and Vicki to join him in the study room. "I know Carl's supposed to be a believer, but isn't it kind of dangerous bringing him here?"

"*Supposed* to be?" Mark said.

"I'm not trying to be difficult," Conrad said. "I just want to be careful."

Mark held up a hand. "I wrestled with the question a long time before I brought him. He's OK."

"I don't like it," Conrad said. "Even if his mark is real, he's still GC. If those guys track him here . . ."

"You were GC before we took you in," Mark said. "Why shouldn't—"

"Want to inspect my mark?" someone said behind them. "Go ahead."

Vicki turned. Carl stood in the doorway. "I don't blame you for being suspicious. Here. See if you can rub it off."

Conrad shook his head. "It's OK. I didn't mean anything—"

"Sure you did," Carl said, walking closer. "What we're doing is dangerous. If the GC find me, I'm dead meat and you guys would be next."

"Which is exactly what I'm saying," Conrad said. "I know how the GC operate. They could easily drag the truth out of any of us if they caught us."

"That's why I don't think I should go back there," Carl said. "There are just too many ways for the GC to—"

"We can talk about the future later," Mark said. "The point is, you're one of us now and you're here."

Carl looked at Vicki. "I want to learn as much as I can as fast as I can."

Vicki nodded. "We'll help you."

Lionel was still asleep when Judd awoke. Judd spent the day watching news reports of the locust attack and reading Tsion Ben-Judah's Web site. He couldn't wait to hear what had happened to Mr. Stein. He imagined the man riding through dangerous territory and giving the gospel in languages he had never even heard of before.

Judd wrote an e-mail about his travels and what he had seen in Africa. He sent it to Tsion Ben-Judah and the kids back at the schoolhouse.

Sam joined Judd and read over his shoulder. When he finished, Sam said, "I've made up my mind. I'm going to see my father."

Judd turned his chair around.

"Don't try to talk me out of it."

Judd scratched his beard. He hadn't shaved in a few days and was surprised at the extra growth. He had tried growing a beard when he was a sophomore without much success. A few of his friends had laughed and made fun of him, but some of the girls thought he looked cute.

"I don't want to talk you out of it," Judd said to Sam. "I think you should go."

"Really?"

Judd nodded. "If your dad hasn't been

stung yet, he will be soon. That may give you a chance to talk with him."

"Shouldn't I try to get to him before he's stung? He can't become a believer afterward, can he?"

"From what I read, it's still possible to become a believer after you're stung—it just won't take away the pain."

Sam sat in thought. Finally he said, "There's a woman who lives next door to our house. She watches the neighborhood like a hawk but stays inside all the time. Maybe she'll know."

Judd took some change from his pocket and handed it to Sam. "Find a pay phone a few blocks from here and call. We'll help you get to him."

"Thanks, Judd." Sam smiled, grabbed the change, and ran out the door.

When Lionel finally awoke, Judd told him the plan.

"You think Mr. Goldberg will be in any mood to talk?" Lionel said.

"For Sam's sake, I hope he's already been stung. That way Sam can talk to his dad and not worry about his dad taking him home."

"I need to talk to you about the deputy commander," Lionel said.

Judd gritted his teeth. "What about him?"

"It seemed like you enjoyed sending that locust after him back at Jamal's apartment. Am I reading it wrong?"

Judd looked away. "I was on the phone when that guy killed Taylor and Hasina. And then he lied—"

"I'm just as ticked off about what he did as you," Lionel interrupted. "Woodruff is a GC scumbag. But you looked like you were doing more than saving Jamal and his family. It looked like you were trying to get even."

"Well, I didn't," Judd said. "The only way to get even with that guy would be to kill him."

"What? You've considered that?"

Judd shook his head. "I haven't told anybody this, but I've thought about it a lot. When I heard what Woodruff did, I made a promise to Taylor and Hasina. If I ever had the chance, I'd try to get that guy back. It wasn't until I heard Woodruff's voice without seeing his face that it all came together."

Lionel ran a hand through his hair. "I don't believe this."

"Maybe I'm wrong for thinking this way," Judd said, "but maybe I'm right. A lot of believers might be spared if he's taken out."

"And what about the 'vengeance is mine says the Lord' stuff? Don't you see? This is the same thing you stopped Taylor Graham from doing when he wanted to shoot Nicolae at the stadium. You're going to get yourself and a lot of other believers in trouble if you try to kill him. And you're going to have to answer to God."

"What do you mean?"

"Ever heard of 'Thou shalt not kill'? I think it's still in effect."

Sam ran in, out of breath. "I talked with her. . . . She said there were droves of locusts around our house. . . ."

"Slow down," Judd said. As Sam caught his breath, Judd explained to Lionel about Sam's neighbor.

Sam continued. "She said that last night a GC ambulance showed up with guys in these weird outfits. They were covered from head to toe with protective gear. They carried my father out and took him to the hospital."

"He's been stung," Judd said.

"Yes," Sam said, "but that's not all. I called the GC hospital and finally talked with a nurse. She wasn't going to help, but I said I was his son. He's on the third floor recuperating from the sting." Sam's eyes widened. "And get this. Deputy Commander Woodruff is in the bed right next to him!"

Judd looked at Lionel. "We'll talk about this later," Judd said.

＊

While the others continued unloading the truck, Vicki and Shelly took Carl into the computer room to begin his training. Lenore peeked in and asked if she could join them while Tolan took a nap. Vicki nodded and Shelly grabbed another chair.

"We'll break this down into three different segments," Vicki began. "First is basic Christian beliefs. You'll need an overview of what the Bible teaches. Second, we'll talk about the prophecies of the Bible and what's coming so you'll have an idea what to expect. And third, we'll talk about how to share your faith with other people."

Carl nodded. Shelly gave him a notebook and he wrote furiously, trying to take down every word.

Vicki began with an overview of the Bible. God had created everything by simply speaking it into existence. He created Adam, then Eve, and had a close relationship with them. Then the people sinned. Since God is holy, he was forced to send the man and the woman away from his presence.

"God's plan all along was to send a savior,

someone who could help restore the relationship between God and people," Vicki said. "That's predicted as early as Genesis 3. Throughout the Old Testament, the coming savior is predicted."

Vicki slowly worked her way through the heroes of the Bible: Noah, Joseph, Moses, David, Daniel, and many of the prophets. She showed Carl passages that pointed to the coming Messiah. She pointed out Isaiah 9: "For a child is born to us, a son is given to us. And the government will rest on his shoulders. These will be his royal titles: Wonderful Counselor, Mighty God, Everlasting Father, Prince of Peace. His ever expanding, peaceful government will never end. He will rule forever with fairness and justice from the throne of his ancestor David."

"Do you know who that's talking about?" Vicki said.

"It sounds like a baby," Carl said, "but then it sounds like God."

Vicki nodded. "It's talking about Jesus. Though he was a man, he's also God. Everyone, every person who has ever lived and every angel ever created, will one day confess that Jesus is Lord." Vicki turned a few pages and showed Carl verses from Isaiah 53.

"Read it out loud," Vicki said.

Carl read, " 'He was despised and rejected—a man of sorrows, acquainted with bitterest grief. We turned our backs on him and looked the other way when he went by. He was despised, and we did not care.

" 'Yet it was our weaknesses he carried; it was our sorrows that weighed him down. And we thought his troubles were a punishment from God for his own sins! But he was wounded and crushed for our sins. He was beaten that we might have peace. He was whipped, and we were healed! All of us have strayed away like sheep. We have left God's paths to follow our own. Yet the Lord laid on him the guilt and sins of us all.

" 'He was oppressed and treated harshly, yet he never said a word. He was led as a lamb to the slaughter. And as a sheep is silent before the shearers, he did not open his mouth. From prison and trial they led him away to his death. But who among the people realized that he was dying for their sins—that he was suffering their punishment? He had done no wrong, and he never deceived anyone. But he was buried like a criminal.' "

Carl looked up. "Whoever this is, it doesn't sound too good for him."

"Throughout the centuries," Vicki said, "most Jewish people thought these two different passages described two people. But now some realize this is the same person you read about earlier. Jesus was both the one who suffered and the Prince of Peace."

Vicki turned to other verses about the sacrifices God required his people to make for their sins. Then she took Carl to the Gospels and showed how clearly Jesus had fulfilled all of the prophecies about the coming Savior. Jesus was killed, buried, and rose again.

"It's all coming together for me," Carl said. "What John told me on the ship and what Mark said made me believe that Jesus was the only way. Now I understand it so much better."

"And there's a whole lot more," Vicki said. She showed Carl verses that clearly taught about the nature of God. He was one spirit, but three persons, Father, Son, and Holy Spirit. She pointed out the depths of God's mercy and love for people, but also that God was holy and required perfection.

"That's why Jesus had to die in our place," Vicki said. "He was the perfect sacrifice for our sins. When we believe in Jesus, God no longer sees all the bad stuff we do. He looks at us and sees the perfection of Jesus."

"Awesome!" Carl said.

Vicki wanted to take a break for dinner but Carl wouldn't let her. "Keep going," he said.

Carl switched hands while taking notes. When his right hand got tired, he switched to his left. "I can use either of them."

Other kids moved in and out of the room while Vicki taught. Pete sat in the corner with Charlie. Conrad and Mark were in another room in a heated conversation.

By nightfall Vicki was again exhausted. She had completed a third of what she thought Carl needed to know. Carl rubbed his eyes and went to the kitchen for something to eat.

"Looks like your student's pretty excited," Pete said.

Vicki shook her head. "He has a lot more energy than I do."

"How long before you think he's ready?"

"Ready for what?" Vicki said.

"To go back to the GC," Pete said.

"Is that why he's so eager?" Vicki said.

Pete smiled. "I think he's eager because he's hungry for the message and he's got a pretty teacher."

Vicki blushed.

"I finally convinced him that we need somebody inside the GC here in the States," Pete said.

"I'm not putting him in that position," Vicki said.

Pete nodded. "And now I'm going to convince you of something."

"Me?" Vicki said.

Pete nodded. "I want you to go south with us."

SEVEN

Carl's Choice

VICKI sat up. She had thought about traveling in the last few days, but she wasn't sure why. Why go anywhere when the kids could reach millions through the Internet?

"You have a gift," Pete said. "The way you explained the Bible to Carl was incredible. You could do that for others."

Mark and Conrad ran into the room. "We just hooked up with Tsion Ben-Judah," Conrad said. "As soon as we get our Web site up, he'll link his site with ours."

"Fantastic," Darrion said.

Vicki pulled Mark aside. "Why were you two arguing?"

"We had a little disagreement about what to call it and what the icon should look like," Mark said. "We'll work it out."

Pete explained his idea to Mark and Conrad. "If Vicki and one or two others come along, you could really encourage some believers."

"What if they're underground?" Mark said.

"That's where Carl comes in," Pete said. "We let the GC ferret out the believers and before they can arrest them, we tip the believers off and give some teaching."

"Won't the GC figure out there's somebody working on the inside?" Conrad said.

"Maybe," Pete said. "Carl will have to be careful."

Vicki chewed on the idea. "How would we buy food or supplies while we're on the road?" Vicki said.

Pete handed her a heavy envelope. "Almost forgot. Z told me to give you this."

Vicki opened it and stared at a stack of bills. She didn't have to count it to know there was enough to last several trips.

"Z said it came from the sale of those coins," Pete said. "He was real happy to pass this on to you. The money from the treasure you guys discovered will probably help believers for years."

Pete paused. "So what do you say, Vicki? Will you go?"

﹡

Judd figured the best route to the hospital for the following day. Lionel and Sam researched locust stings. Using household items they came up with a mixture to put on that looked just like a real sting.

Jamal asked Judd about the plan. Judd explained Sam's concern for his father but didn't mention Deputy Commander Woodruff.

"I'm behind you," Jamal said. "If you need a vehicle, you can use mine."

Nada stayed to herself. Judd had seen her at meals, but they hadn't talked. Judd knew they needed to talk, but now wasn't the time.

Early in the morning, before they left, Judd found an e-mail from Vicki. She brought him up to date on all the changes at the schoolhouse. She asked about Mr. Stein. Then Vicki asked Judd about Pete's proposed trip. Judd's first reaction was to tell Vicki to play it safe. She was finally in a place where the GC couldn't find her.

Instead, Judd put himself in Vicki's shoes. What would he do in the same situation? Judd selected Vicki's last sentence and hit the reply button.

> *<I really value your opinion about this. Love, Vicki>*

Vick,

I only have one thing to say about the trip. Go for it! I wish I were there to go with you. Sounds like God has prepared you to help the people you'll meet.

Lionel and I will try to get back soon. Whenever that is, know that we're praying for you and wish you the very best. Be as careful as you can about the GC and as bold as you can about the gospel.
Love,
Judd

※

By the time Vicki received Judd's e-mail, she was completing her teaching with Carl. He had soaked up the basics of the faith and prophecy the first two days. During the third segment, Vicki brought in several others and had them tell their stories. Shelly, Mark, Conrad, and Lenore told of their experiences. Each story showed a different aspect of sharing your faith.

When Darrion stood, a hush fell over the room. "My story's a lot like yours," she said to Carl. "I had someone who was willing to put his life on the line for me.

"Ryan Daley was in the wrong place and got

caught by some guys who wanted to hurt my dad. But Ryan told me the truth. I didn't want to hear it. I even told him to shut up a couple of times. But he showed what it means to be a true believer. He risked me being mad at him and those other guys trying to kill him just to give me the message."

Vicki looked through tears around the room. All the kids who knew Ryan were crying. The others were silent.

"How did he finally get through to you?" Carl said.

"I thought God was a force in the universe," Darrion said. "I'd meditate and try to work myself into a spiritual state. That was empty. Ryan said God was a person, and when he prayed, he prayed to somebody who cares. That's part of what turned me around and got me thinking that Ryan was right."

"Where's Ryan now?" Carl asked.

Vicki cleared her throat. "The earthquake. He was caught inside a house. He died at a hospital and we buried him near the church where we first heard the truth."

"Sounds like a brave guy," Carl said. "Was he older than you?"

Vicki bit her lip. "He was the youngest of us. But in some ways, he was a lot older."

Phoenix came to Vicki and nuzzled her

hand, almost as if he understood they were talking about his friend.

※

Judd drove Lionel and Sam to the GC hospital where Mr. Goldberg was being treated. Lionel took Judd aside and said, "What about Woodruff? Have you thought more about taking revenge?"

Judd nodded. "I've thought it over. I was wrong to think about taking the guy out. I won't try anything up there."

"Good," Lionel said. He turned to Sam. "How are we going to get clearance to go into your father's room?"

"I have a card that says I'm a family member of a GC employee," Sam said. "If that doesn't work, we'll sneak up."

Judd parked in front of the hospital and the kids put on their act. They moaned and writhed in pain like others who had been stung. GC guards in protective masks and bulky gear guarded the entrance.

"One of us should wait with the car in case we need to make a getaway," Judd said.

"We'll draw straws," Lionel said, tearing two strips of paper. "Shortest goes inside."

Judd drew the shortest. Lionel grabbed

him and whispered, "Any trouble and you're out of there."

Judd and Sam limped toward the entrance. The Global Community had wired an electric shield that zapped any locusts that tried to enter. When Sam spoke with the first guard, Judd couldn't hear the man's muffled response.

"Say again?" Sam said, moaning a little.

"Visitors go to the side entrance," the guard yelled.

The side entrance was a series of doors the GC had rigged to keep the locusts out. Sam and Judd slipped through easily and approached the front desk. A man lifted his visor to look at Sam's ID. He waved Sam through and Judd followed.

"Just a minute," the guard said to Judd. "Who are you?"

"He's my brother," Sam said. "Doesn't have an ID card with him."

The guard waved them on and Sam pressed the elevator button for the third floor.

"Pretty smooth," Judd said.

"I didn't lie," Sam said. "You're my brother in Christ and you don't have a GC ID card with you."

The elevator dinged on the third floor.

"Follow me," Sam said, "and act like you know where you're going."

Judd put his head down and walked briskly behind Sam. He glanced at the nurses' station but they all seemed busy with charts or monitors.

"Three more rooms and we're there," Sam whispered.

"Stop!" someone shouted behind them.

Judd froze. Sam turned and meekly said, "I'm here to see—"

"This is a restricted area," the nurse said. She walked quickly toward them.

Judd stared straight ahead. Sam handed his ID to the woman and said, "It's my father. He's in that room down there. Please let me see him."

"If you two were stung, how are you walking?" the nurse said.

Judd let out a moan and grabbed his neck.

"They were light stings, ma'am," Sam said. "Tiny locusts."

The nurse lowered her voice. "You don't fool me. I know who you are. I see the mark on your forehead."

Judd turned as the nurse pushed up her hat and revealed the mark of the true believer. He sighed.

"I don't know what you're doing here," she said, "but I'd suggest you turn around and get out as quickly as you can. Who are you here to see?"

Sam told her. The nurse shook her head. "This floor is filled with top brass from the GC. Do what you have to and leave. If you get in trouble, I won't be much help."

Sam nodded and limped down the hall-way. Judd followed him into his father's room. The shades were drawn. A curtain surrounded the first bed. Inside, someone moaned in pain.

Judd walked to the head of Mr. Goldberg's bed and stayed in the shadows as Sam approached. Sam took a cool cloth and placed it on the man's forehead. Mr. Goldberg opened his mouth and groaned in agony.

"I bring you greetings from someone who loves you," Sam whispered.

Mr. Goldberg panted. He opened blood-shot eyes and struggled to see. "Who . . . are you?"

Sam knelt by the bed, clearly in anguish. "I'm so sorry this happened, Father."

"Samuel," Mr. Goldberg gasped. He sat up a little and took Sam's face in his hands.

"How do you feel?" Sam said.

He laid his head on the pillow. "They've given me so much morphine I can hardly believe I'm awake. But it doesn't do a thing for the pain." Mr. Goldberg looked at Sam's neck. "They got you?"

Sam hesitated. "No. I put this on to make people think I had been stung. Father, God has spared those who believe in him from this plague."

"You're lying," Mr. Goldberg moaned.

Sam peeled the fake sting from his neck and rubbed away the red coloring. "See? I'm not hurt. I'm telling the truth."

"You chose to leave," Mr. Goldberg said. "Let me die."

"You won't die. This pain will continue for five months, and you'll want to die, but you won't be able to."

"And that is evidence of the love of God?"

Sam drew closer. "Why can't you see I'm telling the truth? Ask God to forgive you."

"I'm already in such pain," Mr. Goldberg choked. "Why must you make it worse?"

"The Bible says if you confess with your mouth that Jesus is Lord and believe in your heart that God raised him from the dead, you will be saved."

"And doing that will take the pain away?"

"No, but it will bring you into God's family and bring us back together."

Mr. Goldberg grabbed Sam's shirt and pulled him close. There was foam at the corners of his mouth and he spit as he talked. "You are one of *them* now. The next time I see you, I will have you arrested."

Sam's lip quivered. "I pray for you every day, Father."

"Get out!" Mr. Goldberg yelled.

Someone grabbed the curtain around the other bed and flung it open. Deputy Commander Woodruff glared at Sam, then glanced at Judd. "You!" he muttered.

Judd kept his back to the wall and slid toward the door. Woodruff reached for something and knocked a metal tray to the floor. He hit a red button and Judd heard an alarm at the nurses' station.

"Father?" Sam said.

"We have to go," Judd said. "Now!"

EIGHT

Trapped

JUDD and Sam burst into the hallway and
narrowly missed a nurse who was rushing to
help. "What's going on?" she said.

"Those guys are in trouble," Judd said.
"Lots of pain!"

Others rushed to the room. Woodruff
screamed, "Get them!"

The nurse who had the mark of the
believer stood at the end of the hall. "Don't
take the elevators. Go up a floor and you'll
find a walkway that leads to the parking
garage. Take the stairs to the ground floor."

"Thanks," Judd said.

"God help you," the nurse said, "and don't
come back."

As Judd and Sam reached the next floor,
GC guards were on their way up. Judd
opened the fourth-floor door and quietly

moved inside. He located the walkway to the garage and ran down the hall.

A radio crackled behind them and a voice came over speakers above their heads. "Security code blue. Security code blue. Secure all exits."

They were ten feet from the entrance to the garage when an electronic signal locked the doors. Judd pushed the handle with all his might, but they wouldn't budge.

"We're trapped!" Sam said.

Judd retreated a few steps and noticed an open door. He and Sam ducked inside as two security guards raced onto the floor.

"Use your passkey to check the garage," one man said. "I'll search the rest of the floor."

Judd and Sam knelt behind a large bin of some sort. The light was off in the room, but the door stayed open enough for them to see. When Judd's eyes adjusted to the dimness, he realized they were in the laundry room. Sheets and towels were stacked in neat piles on shelves. The hampers were full of dirty linen.

Judd glanced around the room and spotted what he was looking for. He closed the door quietly, locked it, and turned on the light.

"We have to work fast," Judd said. "Tie some sheets together as tightly as you can."

"What for?" Sam said.

"Just hurry!"

✳

Lionel sat outside the hospital entrance listening for more news about the locusts. Jamal's car had a shortwave radio and Lionel tuned in reports from around the world. One station played a recording of a reporter in London who was standing on the roof of a building as the locusts descended. The man described the swirling cloud perfectly. Then, with the beat of locust wings growing louder, the reporter realized this was not a weather phenomenon but an attack by beings he had never seen before.

"They're coming now," the man said in his heavy accent, "flying beasts that look like they might be from some horror film. You can hear their wings and a weird chant of some sort."

The soundman for the reporter dropped his equipment and ran, only to be attacked and stung. His cries mingled with the wails of the reporter who also dropped his microphone.

The chilling report brought back the moment Lionel had first seen the locusts. As he flipped to another frequency, he noticed guards talking on radios and scurrying to the visitor entrance.

Lionel flipped off the radio and muttered, "This doesn't look good."

He pulled the car close to the building, parked behind a Dumpster, and got out. Locusts buzzed near closed windows. He walked close and heard the security alarm. *Judd and Sam must be in trouble*, Lionel thought.

He tried the visitor entrance but it was locked. A guard inside waved him away. Lionel nodded and walked around the corner. He saw a delivery truck parked near a service entrance. Lionel recognized the logo. It was a laundry truck.

The back of the truck was open, but there was no one inside. Lionel guessed it had been there since the locusts' attack. Lionel noticed a ring of keys on the ground.

Somebody was in a hurry to get out of here, Lionel thought. He picked up the keys and climbed onto the loading dock. Two doors. A huge one that rolled like a garage door and another smaller one to the side. Lionel fumbled with the keys. If he could find the right key, he might be able to help his friends.

***

Judd and Sam had tied several sheets together when the guard from the parking garage returned. "There's no one in there."

"We have the place locked down," the other man said. "We'll find them."

The guard tried the door to the closet. Judd dived behind the hamper.

"This is locked; they couldn't have gotten in here," the guard said.

When the two walked away, Judd tied the end of the last sheet around Sam's waist. "You're going for a little ride."

"Out the window?" Sam said.

Judd shook his head and walked to a small metal door on the wall. "Down here."

"The laundry chute!" Sam said. "Perfect."

"I'll lower you slowly and you can tell me what you find," Judd said. "Tug it once if things are clear. Tug twice if you want me to pull you up."

"Got it," Sam said. He climbed inside the chute and tried to walk on the metal tunnel. His footsteps echoed.

Judd shook his head again. "Don't walk. I'll lower you."

Judd hoped the sheets would be long enough. He lowered Sam inches at a time, making sure the knots they had tied didn't come loose.

"There's a curve at the bottom," Sam whispered from below. "I can't see anything down here, but I don't hear anything either."

Footsteps in the hall. Keys jangling. Someone said, "What's this door?"

"It's the fourth-floor laundry," a woman said. "We usually keep it unlocked because—"

Sam slipped and banged against the side of the chute.

"Did you hear that?" the man outside said. "Open this door. Now!"

"Let go!" Judd said to Sam.

Sam untied the sheet from his waist and slid out of sight with a thump. Judd quickly tied the end of the sheet to the handle on the chute door and climbed inside. The door closed and it was pitch-dark. Judd slid down, holding the sheets to steady himself. The door to the room burst open. Moments later he felt something tugging. Light from above. A man stuck his head inside. "He's going down the laundry chute!"

The click of a knife. Ripping. The guard was cutting the sheet on the handle. Judd fell and hit the curve in the chute with a terrific crash. Still holding on to the sheet, he flew into a huge hamper and landed in a soft pile of linens. Sam held out a hand. "We don't have much time."

A radio crackled. "They're in the first-floor laundry room," a man said.

"Good," another said, "those doors are on lockdown. We've got them."

"Deputy Commander Woodruff wants them upstairs when we catch them!"

Judd and Sam raced through piles of laundry. Sam stopped at an empty bin and put one leg inside.

"They'll find us if we try to hide," Judd said. "We have to get outside."

Suddenly, a door swung open and light streamed into the room. Sam turned to run but Judd grabbed his arm. "Lionel!"

"Come on!" Lionel shouted.

A few locusts flew inside the open door as the boys raced out. Lionel closed the door and locked it behind him. Seconds later the kids heard voices and pounding on the door.

Judd jumped in the driver's seat and started the car. Lionel and Sam were barely inside when Judd floored it and squealed past the Dumpsters. In his rearview mirror, Judd saw several GC officers in protective gear run into the street.

After he caught his breath, Lionel said, "What happened up there?"

Sam shook his head. "My father would not listen. He's so closed to the truth."

"But he would have let us go," Judd said. "It was Woodruff who sounded the alarm."

Sam stared out the window. "That may be the last time I ever see my father."

Moving to the schoolhouse had been Vicki's idea, so the thought of leaving wasn't easy. Putting it in the hands of others was painful, but she felt it was the right thing to do.

Carl had soaked up the teaching faster than anyone. At the end of each session he peppered her with questions, asking her to clarify certain points.

"If a person rejects the message, what do I do?" Carl said. "Do I just move on to somebody else?"

"Think about what John did for you," Vicki said. "He didn't give up just because you rejected it the first time."

"What about inside the GC compound? They need to hear the message, too, but it'll be risky to talk."

Mark stepped forward. "Each of us has a different role. One person might need to be bold with everyone they meet. Another, like you, has to be careful. We're all working together to see that as many people as possible hear the message."

After each session, Lenore had stayed up late working in the computer room. Vicki asked what she was doing, but Lenore said, "It's a surprise."

When Vicki felt she had covered everything

and Carl had no more questions, the kids packed and gathered in the kitchen. They all agreed to pray for Carl every day and ask God to give him safety as he worked from inside the Global Community.

Mark agreed to stay and take over theunderground-online.com Web site. With Darrion's help, the kids hoped millions from around the world would read the questions and answers they posted in the next few weeks.

Conrad, Shelly, and Vicki would accompany Pete on his trip south. Their mission was to warn the various underground groups of believers who were being targeted by the Global Community.

Lenore volunteered to oversee the schoolhouse. With Charlie's help, she would care for Janie and Melinda, make sure the kids had meals, and keep an eye on the baby, Tolan.

Vicki agreed to keep the others informed with e-mails every few days. They set up an emergency alert system for Carl in case the GC caught onto him. Mark also developed a program that would turn their e-mails into a code that only the kids could read.

Carl pulled out a tiny computer and checked information on GC flights. Since the locust attack, all GC aircraft had been grounded. He sent a message to his superiors and told them he was returning to the base in the next few days.

"I have to make a run back through here every few weeks," Pete said. "I'll make sure these guys get back here as soon as possible."

Lenore approached Vicki with a wrapped package, tears in her eyes. "I made a little something for you."

"You didn't have to do that," Vicki said.

"I can't thank you enough for what you've done for Tolan and me. I'm sure we'd both be dead. And we wouldn't have known anything about God's love."

Vicki began unwrapping the package but Lenore put a hand on her arm. "Wait until you get on the road."

Vicki excused herself and ran upstairs. She wanted to say good-bye to Janie and Melinda, but both of them seemed not to notice her.

When she turned to leave, Janie gasped, "Where are you going?"

"Taking a little trip," Vicki said. "We have to find some people down south."

Janie tried to sit up. She clutched her stomach and fell back. "Bring us some medicine or something for the pain!"

"Try to eat," Vicki said. "You're both going to get skinny if you don't."

Pete pulled out and drove the truck

cautiously along the country road. Vicki opened Lenore's package and found a notebook. She opened it and read, "I took shorthand in college too. I think I got just about everything in here. May God use you mightily in the coming days. Love, Lenore."

Vicki opened the notebook and found her complete sessions with Carl. Every word, all three days, printed perfectly. *So that's what she was working on*, Vicki thought.

NINE

Searching for Believers

VICKI couldn't believe the room in the truck. Pete drove, Carl rode in the passenger seat, and Vicki, Shelly, and Conrad sat behind them in the sleeper. The truck had a satellite hookup for phone and video, an onboard computer, and a citizens band radio. Pete showed Vicki how to access the Internet through the satellite and the kids surfed the Net as the truck rolled through Illinois and Indiana on its way south.

The interstates were a disaster in some places and fine in others. In the more populated areas, GC crews had repaired roads. Other areas hadn't been as hard hit by the earthquake. But nearly every overpass in Indiana had collapsed. Pete would take each exit and return to the highway on the other side of the collapsed bridge.

The road was nearly deserted. Other than a few large trucks and an occasional car, they were alone. "We're going to make good time," Pete said.

The kids picked up satellite reports from GC news sources. Other countries had suffered the same fate as the state of Illinois. Streets were deserted. People suffered. In South Africa, a news van passed a row of houses and a high-powered microphone picked up the howls and sobs from inside. A doctor interviewed in China, who had the mark of the believer, showed beds filled with people who had tried to kill themselves. They drove cars into concrete walls, drank poison, cut their wrists, sat in garages with cars running, leaped into deep water, even jumped from high buildings in attempts to take their own lives. Though some of the patients' bodies were torn and bleeding, not one of them had died.

Vicki turned away from the monitor and watched the passing towns. In Kentucky, horses ran by the road.

"Earthquake destroyed a lot of fences," Pete said. "The farmers almost had them repaired when the locusts came. Now the horses are running wild."

Night fell and Vicki felt the familiar pop in her ears as they climbed the Smoky Mountains. A few years earlier she had traveled with her family in a small RV her father had borrowed from a friend. Her dad wanted to take the family to Orlando to a theme park, but the vehicle had broken down in Georgia. They spent the entire vacation in a little hotel about fifty miles from the ocean waiting for the RV to be fixed.

As she drifted off to sleep in the truck, Vicki recalled how much she had complained about that trip. Her mom and dad weren't Christians at the time and they both drank a lot of beer. The pool at the hotel was the size of a postage stamp, there was no cable TV, and the air conditioner only cooled the room to eighty degrees.

"This is worse than staying home in our trailer!" Vicki yelled one night. "You said we'd see the ocean."

"I said a lotta things," Vicki's father said, "but this is outta my control."

Then the screaming began. The family next door called the manager and the manager called the police. Vicki wound up running out of the hotel and walking a lonely road most of the night. She hated being poor. She hated her parents for messing up their lives. And she hated being stuck in a hot hotel room with her little sister, Jeanni. To make matters worse, Jeanni was having a great time.

The police didn't arrest anyone that night, and the RV was fixed a few days later, but her parents had used all their vacation money on the hotel. They canceled the rest of the trip.

"Please let us go by the ocean," Vicki pleaded as they started their long drive home. What Vicki's father did next shocked her. It still surprised her, just thinking about it. He pulled the RV to the side of the road, backed up, and turned around.

"You kids are gonna get your feet in the Atlantic if it's the last thing I do," he said.

Jeanni had screamed with delight when they saw the water. It was the first time she had seen anything bigger than Lake Michigan. They parked and Vicki took off her shoes and ran to the shoreline, digging her toes in the wet sand. She picked up a few shells and stuffed them in her pocket.

She looked back and saw her mother and father at the RV, shouting at each other. Vicki walked into the water. She wanted to keep going, just walk until the water was over her head.

"What are you doing?" her father screamed, standing by the shore. "Get back here!"

Vicki waded back, a wave toppling her when she turned. Her dad grabbed her arm as she went under and pulled her up, her hair wet with the salty water. Then he smiled.

It had been such a long time since Vicki had remembered her father's smile. The events since the disappearances had kept her so busy she didn't think much about the past. But now, with the rumble of the diesel engine and the shaking of the truck cab, she let herself go back. She remembered little things like her dad's stale beer breath, the brand of cigarettes he smoked, and little Jeanni's screams as Vicki chased her around the house. She remembered the laundry her mother used to hang on a line by the trailer. Seeing one of her shirts or a pair of pants flapping in the breeze always embarrassed Vicki.

But there were moments, even before her mom had believed in Christ, when they sat at the kitchen table and talked. Vicki's mom had shared some of her dreams that would never come true. Vicki tried to listen and say helpful things, but sooner or later another fight would start and her mother would grab a bottle and Vicki would slam her bedroom door.

"Do you want something to eat?" Vicki heard someone say.

"Mom?" Vicki mumbled. She opened her eyes and saw Shelly. They were sitting in front of a truck stop.

"I'm not your mother," Shelly laughed.

"Come on. Sun's coming up. We're in North Carolina. You've been sleeping all night."

The truck stop was almost empty. There was no one healthy enough to work in the diner, so Pete picked out some packaged food and paid for the fuel.

"How much longer?" Vicki said as they sat in a grimy booth at the back of the restaurant.

"We'd be about eight hours away under normal conditions," Pete said. "With the damage from the earthquake and the tidal wave after the meteor, we'll be lucky to get there by nightfall."

While Pete rested in the passenger seat, Carl got behind the wheel. He looked scared of all the gears at first, then seemed to get used to them. Locusts skittered among the trees as they drove through the mountains. Carl slowed as locusts flew toward the windshield. Once they saw everyone's mark, the locusts flew away.

Pete awoke and took the wheel as they crossed the South Carolina border. Ruins of destroyed homes littered the roadside. Tiny shacks with signs advertising shrimp and crabs had sprung up. Then the scenery changed. Through the palmetto trees, Vicki saw the expanse of water she had dreamed about.

"This whole area was devastated by the wave," Carl said. "Changed everything."

"How did the GC keep their military buildings?" Conrad said.

"Most of them were destroyed," Carl said. "Had to be rebuilt from the ground up. A few made it through."

Pete opened his window and an ocean breeze blew through the cab. Vicki closed her eyes. She could almost hear the water lapping at the shoreline.

"Can we stop and get out?" Vicki said.

Pete turned and eyed her.

"It's been so long since I've been in salt water. It'll just be for a minute."

Pete smiled and pulled to the side of the road. A sandy path led through what had been a small park. A crooked teeter-totter and monkey bars were all that remained.

"Enjoy yourself," Pete said. "We'll stay here for the night."

Vicki, Shelly, and Conrad took off their shoes and jogged down the path. They stretched their legs and raced to the edge of the water. Vicki closed her eyes and breathed deeply. She could almost hear her family from years ago. When she looked at the horizon, the sun dipped below the salt marshes and sea oats. The tidal wave had changed what people had built, but it couldn't take away the natural beauty God had created. The sky turned a purplish orange as the sun faded.

Carl came running onto the beach and kicked water at the others. "Pete says dinner's about ready. And good news. We're pretty close to the location where the group I was telling you about is supposed to meet. Thought we'd head over that way a little later and see if we can find anybody."

Pete boiled shrimp and made sandwiches for everyone. Vicki didn't know how to peel the shell off the shrimp, so Carl showed her. Soon the kids were full.

"What's this place called?" Vicki said.

"We're near Beaufort," Carl said. "We'll drive down by the river and you can see some of the old mansions. A few of them are still standing."

"What about the believers?" Shelly said. "You think they meet somewhere near here?"

Carl pulled out a map of the area with a red circle around a nearby town. "The report we had said they met in an old Christian radio station near Port Royal."

Pete helped Carl pull motorcycles from the back of the truck. "I'm bushed. Going to get some shut-eye. You kids be careful."

Carl and Vicki rode ahead of Conrad and Shelly. They found Main Street in Beaufort, and though much of it had been washed away, Vicki could tell how beautiful it once was. Mansions dating back to the Civil War had somehow survived the massive onslaught of water after the meteor. A few shops remained but were darkened.

Carl checked his map again and rode farther south. Spanish moss hung from live oak trees that lined the road. The building was small. Pine needles and branches covered the driveway. When the motorcycles stopped, Vicki heard insects singing their evening song. A light flickered inside the building, then went out. Something scurried in the leaves.

"What was that?" Shelly said.

"Probably an egret or a heron," Carl said. "Most of the deer and the foxes were killed by the wave."

A short-necked bird with red eyes darted overhead. Vicki screamed and jumped back.

"It's just a night heron," Carl said. "It's OK."

Carl walked up the concrete steps and tried the door. It was locked. He knocked softly. Conrad went around the side of the building to look in a window. When no one answered Carl's knock, he called out, "We've come to help you. Let us in."

Conrad shuffled around the corner, his hand behind his back. Behind him was a burly young man. He had sandy hair and arms like tree limbs. He held Conrad's arm with one hand and had a knife in the other.

"Throw down your guns and anything else you got," the boy said, "or this guy's history."

The kids put up their hands. "We don't have any weapons with us," Carl said.

"I know that uniform. You're GC."

Vicki stepped forward. The boy's face was shaded from the moonlight. "Are you a believer?" she said.

"Tom, get a flashlight out here now!" the boy shouted.

Another boy, shorter but just as athletic, opened the door. He shone a light on Carl's forehead and on the rest of the group. The teen holding Conrad let go. "Didn't know we'd have other believers visiting or we'd have cooked you guys some dinner."

"Let me apologize for my brother," the shorter one said. "I'm Tom Gowin. This is Luke. Come in."

The kids shook hands and entered the tiny building. Seven other kids stood in a circle around an old radio transmitter. Vicki loved their accent and was excited to have found other believers.

"We came to warn you," Carl said. "The Global Community knows about this group and has a good idea where—"

"We know," Tom said. "They came here just before the big bugs did."

"They took some of our supplies and dumped the rest in front," Luke said. "I think they were gonna torch the place."

"What happened?" Vicki said.

"Didn't have the chance," Tom said. "Sky opened up and poured some of God's little demons on their heads. Those GC went flyin' outta here. Don't think they'll be back anytime soon."

"They'll be back," Carl said. He explained what he knew about the GC plan to locate and capture believers. "They're targeting people who are spreading the message."

"People like Dr. Ben-Judah," Tom said.

"Right," Vicki said. "But Tsion is safe. The Trib Force won't let—"

"You talk like you know him," Tom said.

"We do," Vicki said, and from the beginning she explained how the kids had been left behind and eventually met the famous rabbi from Israel.

"I can't believe you actually know him," one of the other kids said.

"We read his Web site before the tidal wave hit," Tom said. "Haven't been able to get the computer working since."

"How did you survive the wave?" Conrad said.

"Long story," Tom said. "Had to go inland a couple hundred miles and when we came back . . . well, you can see what happened."

Luke stepped forward. "Can you tell us what's going on with the Tribulation Force? We want to be a part of it, but there's so much we don't know."

Carl looked at Vicki and smiled. "Where's your notebook?"

TEN

Pavel's Plan

AFTER Judd and the others arrived at Yitzhak's house, they hid the car and spent a few days keeping out of sight. As Tsion Ben-Judah had predicted, people were busy avoiding the locusts or were hurting from their stings.

Jamal was concerned for the kids' safety, but he didn't seem as peeved as before. Sam was dejected about his father.

"Your dad could have kicked you out when he recognized you," Judd said. "It was Woodruff who caused the problem."

"God can still get through to your dad," Lionel said. "Just because he was stung doesn't mean there's no hope."

Late one afternoon Judd climbed to Yitzhak's attic to spend some time alone. He took Yitzhak's laptop and logged on to Tsion's Web site. Tsion included many of the stories of the 144,000 witnesses who had gone to remote places. He searched for Mr. Stein's name but couldn't find it.

Judd clicked on theunderground-online .com icon and was surprised to see how much material was already on the Web. He recognized many of the questions and answers. He and Mr. Stein had worked on them a few weeks earlier. Just looking at the material made him long for home and his friends. He wondered if Vicki had gone on the trip and what was happening at the schoolhouse.

He jotted a quick note to Mark and asked for an update, then checked his own e-mail. He found hundreds of messages from kids who wanted answers. He composed a reply and told everyone to check out Tsion's Web site and theunderground-online.com.

As Judd went through rows of messages, one caught his eye. It was from Pavel, his friend in New Babylon. Judd hadn't talked with him in a long time. Pavel's father was a worker with the Global Community and Judd had been thrilled when the boy had responded to the message of the gospel.

Judd opened the message. It read: *I know where you are. Please e-mail me as quickly as you can. I have some wonderful news. Better yet, let's talk by computer link. Pavel.*

Judd set up the laptop's camera and sent a message to Pavel. As he waited, he heard a noise on the stairs. It was Nada.

"Am I disturbing you?"

"Not at all," Judd said. He looked around for a chair.

"I'll sit on the floor with you," Nada said.

Judd explained who Pavel was and that he lived in New Babylon. "Perhaps he knew my brother?" Nada said, scooting closer. She sighed. "Judd, I want to talk about what happened back at my house. My mother says I should move on, but I can't pretend I don't have feelings."

Judd stared at the computer as Nada continued. "I've seen how much you care for your friends. You're willing to risk your life. You've done the same for me. You don't know how hard it was at home, being cooped up, hiding, and taking people in. Then you came. The talks we had were wonderful. I feel like I've known you all my life."

"I enjoyed talking too," Judd said. "We have a lot in common, with our faith and wanting to work against the GC."

Nada grew quiet. Finally she said, "I don't know if I should tell you this. I have prayed about it and I think God wants me to . . ."

"Go ahead," Judd said.

"I think you're running."

Judd laughed. "Yeah, we're all running from the GC."

"No, I mean on the inside. I see it in your eyes. You've told me bits and pieces about your life and it seems you're always on the move. Always flying here or moving around with your friends."

"We've had to stay on the run from the GC—"

"I'm not explaining it well," Nada said.

Judd looked at the floor and nodded. "If you'd have known me before, you wouldn't have liked me. I guess there's still a part of me that's restless."

"I'm wondering if you could ever . . . if before the Lord's return you could be interested . . . in someone like me?"

Judd looked into Nada's eyes. She glanced down but Judd touched her chin and lifted it. "I told you I care a great deal about you. But there are things you don't know. Things even I don't understand."

Judd scooted closer. "God put us together for a reason. I don't know why. Maybe he wants us to . . . to get more serious. Or maybe he just wants us to stay friends."

"I'm twenty and I know that we have almost five years before Jesus will return.

I want us to be more than friends during those years."

Judd nodded. "I understand. I just need some time."

Nada turned away. "That means I'll never hear from you again. You'll go off on some—"

"Stop," Judd said. "It means I need some time. That's all."

Nada stood to leave. A message popped up on Judd's computer. It was Pavel. "Stay," Judd said. "I want you to meet him."

Pavel pushed his wheelchair close to the computer. His voice seemed weak. "Is it really you, Judd?"

Judd introduced Nada and briefly told Pavel what had happened to them since coming to Israel. Pavel couldn't believe all of Judd's travels. "I found out you were in Israel from some of your friends back in the States."

"What's the exciting news?" Judd said.

"My father has become a tribulation saint!" Pavel said, beaming.

"What happened?" Judd said.

"It's a long story. But reading Tsion Ben-Judah's Web site was an important part of him coming to the truth."

"Did he pray before the locusts came?" Judd said.

"Yes, but as you know, he works for the

Global Community and nearly everyone has been stung there. He has had to fake a locust sting in order to not appear suspicious. We also have a safeguard on our e-mail and computer transmissions. He met a believer named David who also works for the Global Community. David helped my father set up this system so it could not be traced."

"What's the word about Nicolae and the ten rulers?" Judd said.

"They're keeping everything a huge secret," Pavel said. "Carpathia and his right-hand man, Leon Fortunato, are in an underground shelter for protection."

"The locusts wouldn't bite Nicolae," Judd said.

"Why not?"

"Too afraid they'd be poisoned."

Pavel laughed, then coughed. His face seemed pale but when Judd mentioned it, Pavel shook his head and continued. "The ten kings and even Peter the Second have been stung. They're suffering terribly."

"With every judgment, Nicolae has turned it into something good for himself," Judd said. "I don't see that happening with the locusts."

"He will try," Pavel said. "My father says Nicole is preparing a televised message for the entire world. He will say the stories of poisonous bites are exaggerated."

Judd laughed. "With everyone suffering? He can't possibly—"

"To convince people, he will conduct his speech with a locust sitting on his shoulder."

"What?!?"

"My father says Nicolae wants to convince people these things can be tamed like pets. But don't believe it. The locust was created with trick photography. Make sure you watch the telecast."

"What a liar," Judd said. "With all the suffering, he's playing games."

"He's not the only crafty one," Pavel said, scooting closer to the camera. "Have you heard about the Christian literature that is flooding the globe?"

Judd nodded. "Lionel told me they helped pack some of it for delivery."

"Nicolae Carpathia has sent his pilots to deliver food and supplies to some of the rulers where people are suffering most. What he doesn't know is that his very plane is carrying shipments of the rabbi's studies in different languages."

"Incredible," Judd said.

"That is the other exciting news."

"You want us to help pack more pamphlets?" Judd said.

"It's not that. It's better. Have you read how Tsion believes this is the time for believers to travel?"

"Sure," Judd said.

"I want you to come here."

"To New Babylon?" Judd said. "How?"

"The pilot of Carpathia's plane, who is also faking a locust sting, is picking up a shipment from Israel in a few days. My father talked with him and explained your situation. The way is clear for you to fly with him and stay at my house. You could possibly get a transport back to the States or anywhere you wish."

Judd could hardly catch his breath. He had seen pictures and videos of the city Nicolae had built, but he never dreamed he would have the chance to see it in person. Before he could answer, Nada quickly stood and walked out of the room. Judd called for her but she didn't turn around.

"Is something wrong?" Pavel said.

Judd shook his head. "We just had a disagreement."

"I assume you'll want to think about the offer," Pavel said.

"Do I have to come alone?" Judd said. "I have two other friends who want to make it back to the States as well."

Pavel adjusted his glasses. "I will speak with my father and get back to you at midnight."

🌿

Vicki retrieved her notebook and was ready to meet with the kids from South Carolina the next day. Pete took Carl south to hook up with the GC and finish his run to Florida.

Pete told Vicki and the others where and when to meet him. "Give me three days and then we'll head north."

Carl thanked the kids for their help and made sure they had access to a computer. "After I get back to the GC, I'll be in touch. Look for my e-mail."

Vicki, Conrad, and Shelly kept the motorcycles and rode behind Luke and Tom's pickup through the lowlands. The smell of saltwater plants was refreshing. They hid the truck and cycles deep in a thicket. Vicki knew she wouldn't be able to find the spot again without Luke and Tom's help.

"What were you guys doing at the station last night?" Vicki said.

"We'd been waiting all day to see who showed up," Tom said. "We put the word out that anyone interested in getting serious about being a part of the Trib Force should be there."

"How'd you know we'd show up?" Shelly said.

"We didn't," Tom said, "but Luke had a dream last night. He was sittin' in a classroom, studying the Bible like nobody's business. I thought he'd had too much shrimp sauce, but he swore it was a message from God."

Luke helped the kids into a small boat. He pushed off and paddled into the middle of the marsh and started the engine.

Vicki turned to ask a question but Luke stopped her. "Just wait, you'll see."

Luke took them through a maze of creeks and small rivers. He knew each sandbar and shallow stream. Twenty minutes later the river widened and it felt like they were headed to the ocean. Luke pulled the boat up to what looked like a tangle of scrub oak and some old logs.

"Who's there?" someone said from behind a tree.

"It's Luke and Tom and some friends," Luke said.

Vicki stepped out of the boat onto dry ground. What had looked like something to avoid from a distance was an actual island with a cabin stocked with food, drinking water, and even a solar-powered computer.

Several people came out of the cabin to greet the kids. Most were teenagers, but a few were a little older. Some, like Luke and Tom, had the mark of the true believer. Others didn't but for some reason hadn't been stung by the locusts.

Everyone crowded around the cabin. Vicki asked questions and discovered most of the kids had lost one or both parents in the disappearances.

"My daddy was a shrimp boat captain," one boy said. "I'd work on the boat all day long when I wasn't in school. The summer before, he tried to convince me to come to his church. He used to drink and cuss a lot, but since he started going there he'd quit doing both.

"He convinced me to go out with him one night, said he had a new plan. I didn't want to go, but he kept after me. He talked about God the whole way and I said I wasn't interested.

"Now, when he was fishing, he always tinkered with something. Nets. The motor. But when we got way out and set anchor, I didn't hear anything. Nothing but the waves lapping at the side of the boat."

"What did you do?" Vicki said.

"I went back to find him, and all that was there were his clothes and his gear. It was the spookiest thing ever. I didn't know if he'd fallen overboard or maybe jumped for some reason. I looked for maybe a half hour before I called a Mayday, but by then things were going crazy. Wasn't too long later that I hooked up with Tom and Luke and they explained stuff to me that made sense."

"Still doesn't make sense to me," a girl said who didn't have the mark.

"That's why these guys are here," Tom said.

Vicki pulled out her notebook and looked at Shelly and Conrad. She took a deep breath. "All that's happened—from the disappearances to the earthquake, the tidal wave to the locusts—has happened because God wants to get your attention."

ELEVEN

Judd's Dilemma

FOR THE next three days, Vicki showed the kids from South Carolina what following God was all about. Shelly and Conrad told their stories and talked with the kids one-on-one.

By the end of the three days, everyone on the island had the mark of the believer. Conrad helped Tom fix their computer and work on the small generator that powered it. Vicki encouraged the kids to read Tsion Ben-Judah's Web site and theunderground-online.com and keep looking for what was coming next.

Luke and Tom took Vicki and the others to meet Pete. As they waited, Luke said, "A lot of what you said we knew, but we didn't know how to tell others. It was a big help watching you explain it."

Vicki promised she would have Lenore put her notes on theunderground-online.com Web site. Pete's truck rumbled in the distance.

"Where are you guys headed next?" Tom said.

"Wherever God takes us," Conrad said.

※

Lionel listened to Judd explain Pavel's plan. At first, Lionel couldn't believe Judd was serious. But the more Judd told him, the more sense it made. The pilot might be able to get them back to the States or know a different way.

"Pavel's supposed to get in touch in a few minutes," Judd said, "but there's something else I need to talk about."

"I hope this is not about Nada," Lionel said. When Judd nodded Lionel said, "Are you crazy? Haven't you learned anything? Jamal's going to—"

"I don't think he's ticked off at me anymore. I think he understands this is between his daughter and me."

"What did she say this time?" Lionel said.

Judd explained the conversation. When he said Nada thought he was restless, Lionel screamed, "I don't believe this! Why are you having the conversation? When she came up here you should have—"

"Fine," Judd said, throwing his arms in the air. "I thought I could talk to you. I thought you could help me work through this."

Lionel took a deep breath and walked to the attic window. "OK, I'm sorry. You're right." He turned back to Judd. "What's keeping you from just telling her that you like her, but you're not interested in anything long-term?"

Judd stared at the computer.

"Why don't you just tell her that you don't feel the same way she does and leave it at that?"

Judd looked up. His eyes were red. "Because it's not true."

"What?"

"My problem isn't telling her I'm not interested. If that were true I could do it. The problem is, I *am* interested."

Lionel sat down hard. He felt light-headed. "Whoa, I didn't expect that."

"Neither did I," Judd said. "I've always thought we'd go back to the States, but this evening it occurred to me that I could stay and work from Israel."

"Man, you've been here way too long," Lionel said. "Sorry, I didn't mean that."

"So, what do you think?"

Before Lionel could answer, the computer beeped and Pavel stared into the monitor. Judd hit a few keys and they were linked.

"I have good news," Pavel said. "My father talked with the pilot and he says he can bring the three of you. But no more than that. I have aliases for all of you. Mac will bring your IDs.

"He will pick you up at Jerusalem Airport as the pamphlets are being loaded. Listen for your names over the loudspeaker and Mac will tell you where to go."

Judd said good-bye to Pavel.

Lionel said, "How can you commit to going to New Babylon when you don't know what you're going to do about Nada?"

"I think we should go see Pavel no matter what," Judd said.

"Nada will think you're running again."

"Maybe," Judd said, "or this might work to confirm what we're both feeling."

※

Vicki sat in the passenger seat and explained to Pete what had happened. He was excited to hear about the new believers in South Carolina and how much help the kids had been.

"Luke and Tom said they're moving their headquarters to the secret island," Vicki said.

"I'm glad you guys got to them before something bad happened," Pete said.

While Shelly and Conrad looked for the latest news on the satellite, Vicki asked about Carl. Pete frowned. "I've been waiting for an e-mail from him. He said as soon as it was safe he'd get in touch and I haven't heard a thing."

Pete had such a load of food and supplies the kids could barely get the motorcycles in the trailer. "Where are we going with all this stuff?" Conrad said.

"Z said there's a group in North Carolina with a storage facility—"

"Hey, hey, I think we have something here," Shelly interrupted. "A message from Carl."

Vicki looked over Shelly's shoulder. "Read it," Pete said.

"It's all garbled," Shelly said.

"It's code," Conrad said. "We have to run it through the program."

Shelly pasted the text into another document and ran the code-breaking program. "OK, here it is," Shelly said. *"Sorry it's taken so long to write. I ran into some trouble explaining how I got back and why I hadn't been stung. The*

GC is major paranoid about the locusts. About 80 percent of the Peacekeepers have been infected. They're trying to keep the other 20 percent healthy and protected with their weird gear.

"My commander asked about the group in Illinois and I told them it was a dead end. I said the people up there were dealing with the locusts just like everyone else. They pressed me about Mark—they knew he was John's cousin—and I said the two were as different as night and day."

"That's true," Vicki said.

"I told him the God stuff doesn't run in the blood like the locust stings and he seemed to buy it."

"I'd been praying Carl would be able to think on his feet," Pete said.

"Listen to this," Shelly said. "The GC are taking the remaining troops that haven't been stung and they're moving them out to several test areas. They're going back to South Carolina. Tell our friends there to stay low the next couple of weeks."

"We'd better e-mail Luke and Tom," Vicki said.

Shelly kept reading. "There are two other hot spots the GC have targeted. One is Johnson City, Tennessee. Don't ask why—they must have reports that the believers there are really strong."

Pete punched in the coordinates for Johnson City on his computer. "We could be there by tomorrow morning if we push it."

"*The other place is Baltimore. I found a memo from the guy who's head of the Enigma Babylon One World Faith there. He's been complaining that a lot of his followers have left. They're reading Tsion Ben-Judah's Web site and some are meeting in a nearby warehouse. All three places—South Carolina, Tennessee, and Maryland—are supposed to get hit Sunday morning.*"

"That's tomorrow morning," Shelly said.

"Those people probably have no idea the GC are onto them," Vicki said. "What about Baltimore?"

"We'll have to go to Tennessee and let someone else figure that out," Pete said.

"There's more," Shelly said. "*I don't have any names in Johnson City, but the believer in Baltimore they're targeting is Chris Traickin. Used to be a senator or congressman before the GC took over. They think he's telling people about God to get them to start a new government. All three of these hits are supposed to be splashed on the news. They want to make these believers an example so it'll discourage others from following Tsion's teaching.*"

"There's got to be a way to get in touch with that Traickin guy," Vicki said.

"I don't understand how the GC can even try this with the locusts still buzzing around," Conrad said. "Write Carl and ask about this suit they're using. Is there any way a locust could get inside?"

"And see if he can get us information on Traickin," Vicki said.

Shelly typed the questions in code and sent it to Carl at GC headquarters. "I'm going to send all this to Mark back at the school-house," Shelly said. "He might be able to find out something from there."

"Good idea," Vicki said.

Pete went as fast as the big truck could go over the crumbling roads. Vicki knew they were racing against time and the GC.

※

The next morning, Judd asked Nada to go for a walk with him.

She frowned. "I thought you were staying out of sight."

"A short walk in the back," Judd said. "Please."

Sam rushed up to Judd. "Lionel just told me about the trip. Thanks for including me."

Judd nodded and excused himself. Nada stared at Judd as they walked into Yitzhak's backyard. A patch of grass led to a rock wall. Up the incline was a waterfall that snaked its way to a tiny pond at the bottom with multi-colored fish swimming beneath lily pads. The water trickled down the rocks.

"You've made up your mind," Nada said. "You're running again."

"Hear me out," Judd said as he lifted her up onto the wall so they could speak face-to-face. "After we talked last night, I realized something. I've known that I care about you a lot, but I didn't know how much until I talked with Lionel.

"I've only been a believer a couple years. My goals are a lot different than they used to be. Now I want to learn as much as I can about God and tell people about him. And I want to make it to the Glorious Appearing, when Christ comes back again.

"In the back of my mind, I've always thought it would be nice to share the pain and the sadness and the few glimpses of joy we get with someone else."

"What are you saying?" Nada said.

"I can see myself staying here."

"What?"

"I never thought I could get used to living outside the States. But living in Israel with your family feels . . . OK. It's good. I could stay, if that's what God wants."

Nada leaned forward. Judd stood on the grass and was at eye level with her. "I want to use this trip to confirm what I feel about you."

"Which is what?"

"I . . . I really like you. Being around you, talking, sharing our faith. I think I might be . . ."

"Will you just say it?" Nada said.

"I might be falling in love. Whoa, that was stupid, wasn't it?"

Nada jumped down and hugged Judd. "It wasn't stupid. It was the most wonderful thing I've ever heard." She pulled away and said, "But I'm afraid this trip will change your mind, or maybe you'll head back to the States and I'll never see you again."

"I wouldn't do that," Judd said.

"We have to make the most of every moment we have together," Nada said. "We don't know what will happen next."

"I agree," Judd said, "and I'm hoping to accomplish two things. I want to confirm my feelings for you and take advantage of the freedom we have while the locusts are loose."

Nada stepped back. "And if I said I didn't want you to go?"

"I have to," Judd said. "Something tells me this will be good for all of us. Maybe I'll get Sam and Lionel a way back home."

"I know I can't talk you out of it," Nada said.

"If things go the way I plan . . . oh no."

"What is it?"

"I'll have to talk with your father—that's how it works, right?"

Nada blushed and smiled. Judd took both her hands in his. "You're going to have to teach me about your culture. You know, what happens when you're dating or engaged."

Nada laughed. "You'll catch on quickly."

Judd leaned close and kissed Nada's cheek. "I love you," she whispered.

※

Saturday evening Vicki checked their e-mail and found a response from Tom Gowin in South Carolina. Tom thanked them for alerting them to the GC activity and said they would pass the word. Mark had also written saying that he had traced the name "Chris Traickin" to an apartment near Baltimore. Mark had tried the phone number repeatedly but there was no answer and no answering machine.

Good work, Vicki wrote. *Keep trying.*

The truck rolled into the night. "How far are we from Johnson City?" Vicki said.

"We just passed Asheville," Pete said. "We could be there in an hour or two, depending on the roads. Question now is, what are you going to do once you get there?"

"Pray," Vicki said. "Pray hard."

TWELVE

A Race against Time

VICKI and the others hit the outskirts of Johnson City, Tennessee, as the sun peeked over the mountain range. Vicki had seen trees and mountains like this in movies, but she'd never seen them this close.

"Just got another e-mail from Mark," Shelly said from the sleeper. "He found somebody who knows Traickin and left a message."

"All we can do is pray Mark gets through to him in time," Pete said.

Pete rolled into a truck stop for a quick refuel and the kids split up to see if they could find any information about the believers in town. The restaurant was nearly empty. Vicki grabbed a stool close to an older man who sat hunched over a cup of coffee. He had long hair that hung past his eyes. Vicki leaned over to reach for a packet of sugar and tried to see his forehead, but the man didn't look at her.

"Nice morning," Vicki said.

The man sipped coffee and grunted, his hands shaking.

"You guys got those locusts around here too. We've seen them everywhere."

The man turned to Vicki and rolled up his sleeve. At the top of a tattoo of an eagle was a huge red welt. The man gritted his teeth in pain. His eyes were bloodshot and it looked like he had been up several nights in a row.

"I'm sorry," Vicki said.

The old man turned back to his coffee and the cook stepped from the kitchen. He wore a soiled apron and a chef's hat. He studied Vicki carefully and said, "What can I get you?"

"A cup of coffee would be great," Vicki said.

As the cook poured the coffee, Vicki said, "You haven't been stung?"

The cook shook his head.

"Why not?"

"Lucky, I guess. Why do you ask?"

Vicki leaned over the counter. "Can you pull that hat back a little?"

The cook smiled. He tipped his hat and revealed the mark of the believer. "How about something to eat? It's on the house."

Vicki moved to the end of the counter, out of earshot of the old man. "I'm looking for a group of believers that meets somewhere in town. Can you help me?"

The cook squinted and pointed toward Vicki's face. "No offense but can I make sure that's real?"

Vicki nodded and the man ran a finger across her forehead. "OK," he said, reaching out his hand. "Name's Roger Cornwell."

Vicki introduced herself and asked about the believers again.

"It's funny—about a half hour ago these two unmarked vans pulled up. Tinted windows. My boss stays inside his glass booth over there. I'm the one who goes outside since he thinks locusts don't sting people who work in the kitchen." Roger snickered.

"The people in the van were believers?" Vicki said.

Roger shook his head. "Don't think so. The driver talked to me through this little speaker mounted by the windshield. Told me to fill up the vans and slid some money through a slot by the door handle. I started to clean the windshield and get a look inside, but the guy told me not to bother. I did see a stack of guns near the side door."

"There were two vans?"

Roger nodded. "And locusts were buzzing around the things like bees to a hive."

"They were GC," Vicki said.

"That's what I thought," Roger said, "but I couldn't figure out why they were way out here. We don't have any militia—"

"It's not about the militia," Vicki said. She explained what they had learned about the GC plan.

Roger nodded and looked at his watch. "The GC must know where we meet. It's a bowling alley on the other side of town. People might already be there praying."

"Can you contact anyone and call the meeting off?" Vicki said.

Roger scowled. "We're talking hundreds of people. Some have e-mail, but mostly we pass along information at the weekly service."

"What about a phone?"

"Phone lines are down out there."

Roger scribbled directions on a napkin. Vicki grabbed it and ran to the truck.

※

The departure time for Judd, Lionel, and Sam was changed to late afternoon in Israel. Yitzhak drove the boys to the airport and prayed for them. Judd was surprised that Nada hadn't come, but she said she didn't like good-byes and would see Judd when he returned.

The names Pavel gave them were called

over the loudspeaker and Captain Mac McCullum met the boys in a VIP room. He was all business until the door closed and they were alone. Mac shook their hands warmly and told them what to expect once they boarded the plane.

"Our space is a little limited with all the materials we're carrying," Mac said. "The cargo hold is full, so we're putting some of the boxes of pamphlets in the main cabin."

Judd led the way onto the tarmac when the time came to board. He had never seen a plane outfitted with so much leather.

The last of the materials were being loaded as Judd and the others were seated. "I'll call you to the cockpit once we're in the air."

The takeoff was flawless, and as Mac said, he called the boys into the cockpit after the plane reached its flying altitude. Judd and Lionel were full of questions.

Mac explained that he had taken over flying the plane from Rayford Steele. "Ray knew it was only a matter of time before the potentate had him killed. He decided to bolt during the Meeting of the Witnesses, then came back and flew Tsion and Chaim home."

"What about Buck?" Judd said.

"He's still stuck in Israel," Mac said. "And it's a shame. He needs to get home to his wife."

"That's right," Lionel said. "Chloe's having a baby soon."

"It's still a few months out, but we're working on a plan that'll get him back in time for the delivery."

"How are you getting us into the country without anyone being suspicious?" Sam said.

"Pavel's dad worked it out," Mac said. "He'll pick you up and drive you to his place. I'm off to deliver some more of the potentate's pamphlets."

Mac laughed. It was wonderful to hear someone laugh again. "I'd like to see old Nicolae's face when he finds out what his personal plane was used for."

"They know the stuff is getting out there, right?" Lionel said.

Mac nodded. "Leon and Peter the Second are furious about all the stuff that's flooding the globe. Those of us who are believers are really in a tight spot. There have been executions already."

"What?" Lionel said.

"A couple of Peter Mathews's staff mentioned something Peter thought was private. They were killed the same day. Carpathia sent Peter a note of congratulations."

Judd shook his head. "No telling what they'd do if they found out you're a believer."

"Exactly," Mac said, "and it might be soon that I have to reveal myself."

"What do you mean?" Lionel said.

"Leon doesn't think we need religion anymore since we have Nicolae to worship. He wants to pass a law that people have to bow when they come into Nicolae's presence."

"That's crazy," Lionel said.

"Just shows what kind of trouble we're in," Mac said.

"Which is why I don't understand why you'd take this kind of chance with us," Judd said.

"I argued with Pavel's father about this little joyride," Mac said, "but this one goes all the way to the top. Some people heard about his son and the condition he's in. They OK'd it so I couldn't say no."

"What condition?" Judd said.

"You didn't hear?" Mac said. "Pavel is . . . well, let's just say the disease that put him in that wheelchair is winning."

"He's going to die?" Judd said.

"I'm sorry you had to hear it from me," Mac said. "I thought you knew."

Vicki told Pete and the others what she had learned. Pete punched in the location of the meeting place and shook his head. "We're about forty-five minutes away if we take my rig."

"Roger showed us a back way," Vicki said.

"I'll get a bike," Conrad said.

Pete ran inside the truck stop and returned with Roger. Conrad rolled a motorcycle down the ramp and gassed up.

"You stick with Pete and help him navigate," Vicki said to Shelly. "We'll see who gets there first."

Vicki grabbed the directions and hopped on the back of the motorcycle with Conrad. Pete and Roger unhooked the trailer.

"What's he doing?" Vicki shouted.

"Maybe he can get there faster without that big load," Conrad said.

Vicki pointed the way as Conrad weaved through back roads. As Vicki suspected, they passed few cars. Some were parked in ditches along the main highways. Vicki guessed these were people who had been driving when the locusts attacked.

"It should be on the other side of this mountain," Conrad said as he turned onto a dirt road that seemed to go straight up.

Vicki held on tightly as they climbed the rutted road, bouncing their way to the top. The only thing more frightening than going up was coming down. Conrad rode the brakes, but it felt like Vicki's stomach was doing flip-flops.

When they neared the bottom, Conrad slowed and turned off the engine. They coasted the rest of the way and came to a stop near a paved road.

Vicki stood on the backseat and craned her neck. She saw the long, white building with a bowling pin on the front.

"Hide!" Conrad whispered. "We've got company."

Conrad pushed the cycle behind some bushes. Two white vans slowly passed and moved toward the bowling alley.

"They're going the wrong way," Vicki said.

The vans drove about a half mile and parked overlooking the bowling alley. "They're probably going to wait until everyone's inside, then spring their little trap," Conrad said.

Vicki and Conrad walked closer to the vans, making sure they kept out of sight. Locusts swarmed around the windows. Every few minutes the drivers activated a spray that sent the locusts scattering. Moments later, the locusts were back, trying to get inside.

From this spot above the valley, the GC could see every car and person who walked inside. Fifty cars lined the parking lot and more were coming every minute.

"How are they going to get all those people into custody?" Vicki said. "There's no way these two vans can hold them."

"Maybe they're bringing in buses once they bust them," Conrad said. "Or maybe they don't plan to take them into custody at all."

"What do you mean?"

Conrad looked at Vicki. "Maybe there won't be believers left alive after they're through."

Vicki shuddered. "That guy at the truck stop said he saw a stack of guns inside."

"Come on," Conrad said, "let's cut across the field."

Vicki nodded and they made their way down the hillside.

🌟

Judd reeled at the news that his friend was going to die. *Why didn't Pavel tell me?*

Mac's information about the Global Community brought Judd back to the conversation.

"That's why those of us who are believers have to stay together and look out for each other," Mac said. "Carpathia and Leon are plotting against Mathews. I've heard the whole thing and it's ugly. It's just like Tsion said in one of his e-mails. This is not just a war between good and evil, it's also a war between evil and evil."

Lionel asked Mac how he became a believer and Mac quickly told the story. Rayford Steele had been there shortly after he had prayed.

"We're heading for some dark clouds up ahead," Mac said. "Maybe you guys had better head to the back and buckle up. We'll talk after we get through this."

Lionel opened the cockpit door and gasped. "I don't believe it. Judd, you'd better come see this."

※

Vicki and Conrad rushed inside and saw people sitting in chairs and even in the bowling lanes. One by one they took turns praying over the sound system. A man came up to Vicki and looked at her forehead.

"If you're a believer, you're welcome," the man whispered, "but the meeting won't begin for another hour. We spend this time—"

"You have to get out of here," Conrad said. "The GC are onto you."

"What?"

Conrad pulled the man inside what used to be a bar. He pointed out the window. "Two vans are filled with Global Community guards. They were sent here to arrest you, or worse."

The man smiled. "Even if there were GC guards up there, the locusts would take care of them."

"They have special suits to keep the locusts out," Vicki said.

The man checked their marks again and said, "You kids aren't from around here, are you?"

Vicki sighed. "Illinois. But we're wasting time. Who's in charge?"

The man stiffened. "Listen, I know you mean well, and as I said, you're more than welcome—"

Vicki ran for the front of the building. A woman was at the microphone in the middle of her prayer. She stopped when Vicki jumped over the front desk.

"Amen," Vicki said. She looked out over the audience. People were streaming through the front door. "I'm sorry to interrupt, but you have to listen."

Vicki's heart beat furiously. "A friend of ours told us to warn you. There are two vans filled with GC guards on the hill. They're waiting—"

"That's enough!" the man with Conrad said, grabbing the microphone.

"Let her talk," another man said, stepping

forward. He looked at Vicki and Conrad and asked their names. Vicki told him, then explained what Carl had told them.

People hurried for the doors. The man put a hand in the air and said, "Hold on. If those are GC, we can't leave at once."

"What do we do, Pastor?" a young man yelled from one of the lanes.

Others echoed, "Yeah, what do we do?"

"First we're going to pray for those people in Maryland. Then we're going to ask the Lord to show us exactly what we should do."

✺

Judd pushed Lionel aside and walked into the cabin of the airplane. A box of pamphlets was open, a few pieces of paper littered the floor. Someone knelt to pick them up.

Judd's heart sank.

"Hi, Judd!" Nada said.

✺

Vicki wiped away a tear as the pastor finished his prayer. A few more people entered the bowling alley and asked what was going on. The pastor asked everyone to sit.

"I don't think we have time to wait," Conrad said.

The pastor nodded. "We need to do something fast. That's true. But if we—"

The alley fell silent. Vicki shuddered at the sound outside. Rumbling. Air brakes. The noise shook the building.

"They're here," Vicki said.

ABOUT THE AUTHORS

Jerry B. Jenkins (www.jerryjenkins.com) is the writer of the Left Behind series. He is author of more than one hundred books, of which eleven have reached the *New York Times* best-seller list. Former vice president for publishing for the Moody Bible Institute of Chicago, he also served many years as editor of *Moody* magazine and is now Moody's writer-at-large.

His writing has appeared in publications as varied as *Reader's Digest, Parade,* in-flight magazines, and many Christian periodicals. He has written books in four genres: biography, marriage and family, fiction for children, and fiction for adults.

Jenkins's biographies include books with Hank Aaron, Bill Gaither, Luis Palau, Walter Payton, Orel Hershiser, Nolan Ryan, Brett Butler, and Billy Graham, among many others.

Eight of his apocalyptic novels—*Left Behind, Tribulation Force, Nicolae, Soul Harvest, Apollyon, Assassins, The Indwelling,* and *The Mark*—have appeared on the Christian Booksellers Association's best-selling fiction list and the *Publishers Weekly* religion best-seller list. *Left Behind* was nominated for Book of the Year by the Evangelical Christian Publishers Association in 1997, 1998, 1999, and 2000. *The Indwelling* was number one on the *New York Times* best-seller list for four consecutive weeks.

As a marriage and family author and speaker, Jenkins has been a frequent guest on Dr. James Dobson's *Focus on the Family* radio program.

Jerry is also the writer of the nationally syndicated sports story comic strip *Gil Thorp,* distributed to newspapers across the United States by Tribune Media Services.

Jerry and his wife, Dianna, live in Colorado.

Dr. Tim LaHaye (www.timlahaye.com), who conceived the idea of fictionalizing an account of the Rapture and the Tribulation, is a noted author, minister, and nationally recognized speaker on Bible prophecy. He is the founder of both Tim LaHaye Ministries and The Pre-Trib Research Center. Presently Dr. LaHaye speaks at many of the major Bible prophecy conferences in the U.S. and Canada, where his nine current prophecy books are very popular.

Dr. LaHaye holds a doctor of ministry degree from Western Theological Seminary and the doctor of literature degree from Liberty University. For twenty-five years he pastored one of the nation's outstanding churches in San Diego, which grew to three locations. It was during that time that he founded two accredited Christian high schools, a Christian school system of ten schools, and Christian Heritage College.

Dr. LaHaye has written over forty books, with over 30 million copies in print in thirty-three languages. He has written books on a wide variety of subjects, such as family life, temperaments, and Bible prophecy. His current fiction works, written with Jerry Jenkins—*Left Behind, Tribulation Force, Nicolae, Soul Harvest, Apollyon, Assassins, The Indwelling,* and *The Mark*—have all reached number one on the Christian best-seller charts. Other works by Dr. LaHaye are *Spirit-Controlled Temperament; How to Be Happy Though Married; Revelation Unveiled; Understanding the Last Days; Rapture under Attack; Are We Living in the End Times?;* and the youth fiction series Left Behind: The Kids.

He is the father of four grown children and grandfather of nine. Snow skiing, waterskiing, motorcycling, golfing, vacationing with family, and jogging are among his leisure activities.

The Future Is Clear

Check out the exciting Left Behind: The Kids series

BOOKS #21 AND #22 COMING SOON!

Discover the latest about the Left Behind series and complete line of products at

www.leftbehind.com